Larry

Enjoy the adventure

S Mary Scott

Abbey's Still

By S. Mary Scott

Œ

Strategic Book Publishing and Rights Co.

Strategic Book Publishing and Rights Co.
12620 FM 1960, Suite A4-507
Houston, TX 77065
www.sbpra.com

ISBN 978-1-61204-999-1

Prologue

On December 18, 1917, the House of Representatives passed the 18th Amendment, following a great deal of pressure that had been put on lawmakers as a result of the Temperance Movement. The amendment was certified as ratified on January 16, 1919, after having been approved by thirty-six states. The 18th Amendment prohibited the manufacture, sale, and transportation of liquor in the United States. The law went into effect on January 20, 1920, one year after the ratification. By that time, some states had already enacted statewide prohibition even before the amendment had been ratified.

There was a wave of dismay in America caused by the enforcement of Prohibition, which in turn led to the growth of organized crime, as illegal means were found to respond to the public demand for alcohol. The effects of this law, which was ultimately repealed thirteen years later, were far-reaching and remain an important part of United States history.

Special Thanks

During the construction . . .

I 'd like to dedicate this book to the friends and family who helped in the building of this book; without their support and faith in me, it would have not gotten done: Rich Rees, Mike Doyle, Nancy Davies, Diane Scott Adams, Kim K., Mark Sample, Emy Lou Snyder, Kathy and Gary Dimas, and Marjean Nelson for their support and never letting me think that it couldn't be done.

❖

Chapter One

Present Day

S he glanced into the rearview mirror as threatening skies seemed to be chasing her down. It had been a long journey, and she was glad to be heading home. Melissa was on the last leg of her drive, entering the busy Schuylkill Expressway from the scenic Pennsylvania Turnpike. The traffic slowed at a mountain curve. Memories of being close to home swept over her, and then she returned to the present with an overwhelming sense of anticipation. Was she doing the right thing by moving back? Where would she work now? She posed questions to herself that had no answers.

Ahead, the traffic slowed to a crawl. She entered a curve with steep rock inclines on one side and the sparkling Schuylkill River on the other. The sculling teams were bringing their slim crafts into the picturesque antique boathouses along the river as ominous skies lent a backdrop to the scene. The road slowed again to a sluggish speed. It had been such a long trip. She just wanted to get there!

As the remnants of a sunny day hugged the skyline of the city, giant dots slammed the windshield, and she clicked a switch on the column and watched as the wipers gradually came to life. The rain only lasted a few minutes—a precursor to the impending storm. Rush hour approached and she decided to bypass the interstate and follow one of the area's oldest and longest back roads. The coming storm would only make a mess of the already messy rush-hour traffic.

"A few more minutes of this trip won't matter," she exhaled slowly, feeling the exhaustion in her voice. "I should enjoy the scenery, the changes. The traffic can only get worse on the interstate."

Route 611, which started out as Broad Street in downtown Philadelphia, used to be the main road there before Interstate 95 was built. The road cut through the heart of the city and up into the northeastern suburbs of Philly. George Washington and his troops had marched up this road many times. Barges, filled with dry goods, were pulled by horses through miles of canals that bordered the road. The old route was slower-paced, but so much more scenic than the highway.

The rain had stopped for a moment, and before long, sights and smells tempted her as she paused at a light while gliding through downtown Philadelphia. Garlic and street steam from the light rain that had fallen wafted in through the open truck window. She remembered Karen and herself as teenagers, tooling around South Street on Friday nights, watching the parade of punk rockers. She'd practically dragged the conservative Karen into Zipperhead, a punk rock clothing store, when they were still in high school. Mel enjoyed the punk culture; there was such brashness to it.

A few times she'd towed Karen over the bridge from Jersey to the Italian Market on Ninth Street. Melissa had loved looking at the wide varieties of food. It had heightened all of her senses to explore the exotic essence of the spice shops, the tang of the meat shops, the aromatic cheese shops, and the kitchen store. Karen always got a cannoli and a cappuccino and Mel would experiment with an exotic tea. Mel would flirt with the produce guys and Karen would shy away. The two of them would sit on benches in front of the produce vendors and sip their hot drinks.

Karen would tell Melissa what her true love Adam did that week. Mel would tell her about another recipe that she had formulated.

Melissa thought that she should stop and see the old Italian Market on Ninth Street once again and wondered if it was still the same. She imagined that they still praised Sylvester Stallone, who ran the streets while making Rocky movies. There was a shrine to former Mayor Frank Rizzo painted on the side of a bakery, and his spirit still protected the tight neighborhood.

Karen was happy just staying at home. Not me, the gypsy, Mel thought. She was always tugging her friend around, even before Melissa got her driver's license. As juniors in high school, they would walk around town. "Now," she sighed, "she is dragging me home to settle down." Travel exhaustion was beginning to settle in her shoulders, and she reached down to take a sip from some cold coffee she had purchased hours before.

Heading north of town, she remembered moving her brother Dan out of Northeast Philly and into a big house over the bridge into Jersey. He's so much happier there now, she thought, even though he has to commute into the city every day.

She flicked on the radio and tuned in to 93.3. Her favorite radio station from long ago, regular old fashioned rock music, played through the loaded-down Ford Explorer, and she kicked up the wipers a notch as the rain began to return a steady rhythm.

The weather report on 93.3 announced that a Nor'easter was approaching the area. From Dover, Delaware, to the Bucks County line, there would be high winds, and an area flood watch had been posted. Winds up to forty miles an hour were expected.

Blah, blah, blah, she thought, this storm is nothing compared to the hurricane that hit the Galveston coast a few days ago. That beautiful shoreline was hard to say goodbye to, she remembered with a long sigh. The storm had kicked up large waves in the usually calm gulf. It reminded her of the ocean and why it was time to head home. Melissa hit the CD button, finishing up the fifth disc of *Kay Scarpetta, Coroner and Investigator* while she headed through the Mayfair section, north of the city.

I remember a bakery around here, she thought, placing her forefinger to her cheek and tapping. They used to sell the best Babkas, she recalled. I wonder if that kielbasa butcher is still open.

She deftly flipped open the book and flicked the sixth CD of *Blow Fly*, a novel by Patricia Cornwall. The hum of the narrator was soothing as Mel maneuvered in the hastily altering rush-hour traffic and the swiftly changing weather. Many of the commuters had turned off into development driveways, and the traffic slowly lessened as the skies grew more ominous. Scarpetta was in pursuit of a killer when Mel hit the pause button, cutting Doctor Kay Scarpetta off in mid-sentence. Just as the wind pushed down hard upon the loaded SUV, she dialed her cell phone to let Karen know she would be there in the next hour.

"Where are you now?" Karen asked.

"I'm just coming up 611 now, above Mayfair."

"Are you hungry?"

"Like you gotta ask—the last time I stopped was before the Lehigh Tunnel."

"Well, you know my cooking," Karen worried, then chuckled. "It's not gourmet like you're used to!"

"Mac and cheese is fine," Mel assured.

"How did you know? That's really all I've got, I wanted to leave the food shopping up to you!"

Karen giggled. "I don't need to tell the great adventurer to be careful, do I? This storm has already robbed Dover and parts of Maryland of power."

"I can't wait to see ya, K; can't wait, ol' sock, ol' kid, ol' pal," Mel mused in a city twang.

"Be careful, Lissa. It's going to get worse! Bye," Karen mothered and was gone.

Mel held the wheel with her knee for a second and pulled a rubber band from her hair, then vigorously shook her curly brunette locks. Karen was the only one that called her Lissa. It set her apart in high school from the other dozen Melissas in school. In the past few years, people had started calling her Mel. That was okay with her, since it was a predominantly male environment that she worked in. She learned a long time ago that in order to make it as a chef, she had to talk like the men and be as tough as them. She had built up a lot of stamina over the last few years. Being a chef required many long hours of work and precise cuts and seasonings. In a hotel, a convention had to be fed three times a day. Conventions could run from fifty people to thousands. Breakfast for one thousand would start at 6:00 a.m. with several racks of bacon. Gallons of eggs had to be poured into giant electric frying tilt skillets, while pounds of home fries were flipped on a huge grill. The rest of the day was spent prepping for lunch and dinner.

She punched the pause button. Kay Scarpetta, coroner, was analyzing evidence. The rain was now gushing down in torrents and the early evening sky had turned a menacing dark grey. She approached the turn on to Marenstein Road that led her out to old Route 32. Old canals still ran along the river, and Route 32 ran with them as it did at the turn of the century and before. The canals looked as if they were already swelling to overflowing. The Delaware River, in the backdrop of the canals, seemed to be picking up momentum. It was hard to imagine that this river was a major form of transportation in the past. Farmers would have horses pull barges down miles of canals to where the Delaware River ran more calmly.

The driving was getting more challenging as the rain hammered on.

"Cool, lightning and thunder; really cool," Mel praised aloud to no one. She remembered when she worked at an Omni Hotel in Oakland, California. A thunder and lightning storm had come through, and her coworkers were afraid and bedazzled at the same time. She hadn't considered the fact that something so familiar to her could be so foreign to another. The other kitchen workers had piled out onto the loading dock to watch the storm in amazement.

There's the road! she thought, and she dug out the map that Karen had emailed her. Three Rhoades Road—unusual name, she mused.

"Yup, a left at the Wawa Dairy Store, on to Three Rhoades Road," she spoke. "It's just a few more miles on the right." The rain, already heavy, picked up another notch, and the wind was rocking her SUV back and forth now. She slowed her pace dramatically and put both hands on the wheel. Just two miles up the road and Kar said she would see a big pastel Second Empire house on the right.

A bolt of lightning flashed behind the house, which sat high up on the land. A loud crack—so close! Then another strike hit a tree right behind her, lighting up the interior of the truck. She had sat bolt upright at the sound, then watched in the rearview mirror as the tree slowly toppled, gaining speed and momentum until it slammed onto the road just behind her. The noise was loud and reverberating. She couldn't believe it—the tree was lying across the road, and she had just passed that very spot only a second before!

Soon the force of the wind shocked her back to her driving duties. Karen wasn't far; she could make it. My non-drinking friend better have something strong, she thought with a long shiver and a sigh that seemed to be filled with tired road dust from the long day.

❖

Chapter Two

Present Day

Karen knew her friend had no fear. She had been on enough adventures with her when they were young. She had spent many hours talking with her about the new boyfriends and new cities she was exploring. Karen would tell of her adventures raising her children. Lissa was there for each of the four births—if not in person, then in spirit. She was the kind of friend she could call in the middle of a frustrating night while holding a sick kid. She was the one she could call after a long day of mommy-ing just to hear the details of her life—the new boyfriend, an unusual menu, or a convention that was in town. The boxed macaroni and cheese was done gourmet style for Mel. She had added some chunks of ham to the concoction and a teaspoon of salsa. A private little joke for this fancy award-winning chef. Maybe now she would stick around for a while. Even a gypsy has to settle down sometime.

She was peering out the sidelights at the front door. Karen was jolted by the closeness of that last lightning strike. She opened the door and went out to the portico to watch. The rain was almost horizontal, and she was getting wet. The full storm was definitely upon them now. The light of a strike illuminated enough for Karen to see a tree come crashing down. She also noticed Lissa's truck just a few yards ahead of it.

The lights dimmed, made an effort to brighten again, and then darkened. Turning away from the door, she ran to grab a flashlight from the hall table. The SUV was coming up the drive.

Just then a tall six-foot guy wearing a tight black tee shirt and faded jeans appeared on the landing behind Karen.

"The TV is out. Do you want some help?"

"I've got more candles in the kitchen drawer. Can you get them and some plates to put them on? It should be my friend from Texas coming up the driveway. I also have flashlights in all of the bathroom closets.

"She still has that old truck!" A smile broadened over Karen's round face as she pushed up her glasses in the process. At least something was constant in her life, she thought as she rushed out to retrieve her friend.

"Hey, stay there; it's too wet!" Mel yelled to her friend standing under the portico, and she grabbed her purse and overnight bag. She made a mad dash to Karen. She dropped her stuff just inches inside the door and gave her friend a big, very long hug.

Tristan found a candle lighter in a drawer with tons of candles. Karen was so organized, he reflected.

"Mmm," Tristan murmured, spying the big pot of macaroni and cheese dinner with the flashlight. No pizza tonight; dinner is made, he thought, grabbing a few saucers for the candles. He lit a few in the kitchen. He came back into the living room with an armful of candles and plates just as Karen was being engulfed by a pretty, medium-size brunette. Some of the curls were sticking to her face as she embraced Karen. She was a mess from the shower of rain, but she had the deepest colored lips he'd ever seen. Her body seemed to engulf his long-time friend. As she looked up they caught eyes, and he stared at her from the shadows of the living room. His heart missed a beat and sent a wave of vibration right through him. What the hell was that, he questioned silently to no one.

Mel looked up as Karen turned and said, "Mel, this is Tristan Knapp—he's staying here with us. I told you about him over the phone."

"Sho' nuff, you did," Mel drawled. "Mighty fine to meet you, Tristan."

"The power went out just as you came up the road. It's just like you to blow into town," Karen reflected.

"Did you see that tree come down across the road? It just missed me! Sure glad I didn't stop at the dairy store for a coffee. It might have hit my truck," Mel banged out without a trace of Texas drawl.

"Are you okay?"

"Forever the worrier, Kar; I'm cool."

"Hey, how about a nice candlelight dinner?" Karen asked, her smirk pushing up her eyeglasses.

"Got any wine? Or a beer, maybe?" She looked over at Tristan, knowing her friend didn't. "Long ride today. I can taste the road dirt," she said, happily picking up her bag.

Tristan finished his candle-lighting ceremony as Karen pushed Mel into the kitchen. Mel showed her how to light a gas stove without electricity. The table was set and a bottle of wine was cracked open. Mel made Karen endure only one glass since she knew her friend was barely a drinker. The three of them called the tree and electricity outage in to the proper authorities and settled around the table with gourmet conversations and gourmet mac and cheese. It was almost nine o'clock when the power was restored.

Tristan got up and turned the lights back off. He was enjoying the candle glow in Mel's eyes. He liked watching her talk about people whom she had encountered around the country. He could see why these two oddball friends got along so profoundly. Karen did everything by the book. Mel, he was finding out, liked to write her own chapter. Mel had no reins and would push the limits till they squeaked, he surmised. She seemed to have no fear, which made her a lot of fun to listen to. He spoke only a few times, trying to let these two friends catch up. He was trying not to stare at this new person, but her eyes and that crooked smile were getting to him. It was all so mesmerizing. Who was this girl? Where did she come from?

Karen was impressed by Tristan's intentness. She had never seen him like this before. He was usually taking off on his own adventures. Some days she didn't even notice him around. Maybe it was the wine. He had cracked a second bottle a half an hour ago when the lights came on. Where did that wine *come* from? Did Tristan have it hiding in his room? Karen deliberated while listening to Mel and picking at crumbs on the table. She was so happy to have her gypsy back with her.

Mel raised her arm to cover a yawn as her eyes closed without effort. She combed through her hair with her fingers, trying to revive herself.

"I'm usually up way later than this," she apologized. "It must have been all of the driving. It was like seven hundred miles that I covered today."

Yet they talked on for another hour before heading up to bed.

She awoke to absolute quiet, except for a distant buzzing of chainsaws coming from outside. She lay there, looking out at the view of woods that careened up a hill. Turkey hawks circled around a tree that had come down on the edge of a hill. Rolling over, she sat up and realized that it was nine o'clock. Damn, I never sleep this late! she thought. She searched the floor, looking for a pair of pants to put on. She had slept in her tee shirt and bra.

"God, I need a shower and a Wawa." She giggled with the thought of this homestyle coffee treat, scratching her side and smoothing out her long wild curls. "I need to unpack my truck. I need to find Karen. I need to check out Karen's house. I need to call my brothers. I need to figure out what to do for a living. *And* I need coffee."

Mel's many years of moving had taught her a lot about houses. She always searched for old houses that had been converted into apartment buildings to live in. These apartments usually came furnished and gave the rented living space a homey feeling. This crusade created a hobby for her of exploring old houses.

She once dated a carpenter for a while. He had taught her a lot about wood and details, showing her where walls had been and illuminating her about basement beams, general construction, and what they told about an old house. She had also learned a little about plumbing and building furniture from a couple of guys she had dated. She used to explore abandoned houses on roadsides all over the country. She had learned the various styles of houses from an old bartender friend.

Her father once owned a fancy Queen Anne Victorian in a historic town in South Jersey when she was in high school. Her Grandma Simone lived in a Second Empire duplex in the university section in Philly. It had a backstairs, a lot of secret rooms, and a big foreboding basement. That house was most likely the inspiration of her exploring hobby.

Mel found Karen on the floor in the living room, patching a hole in the woodwork made by a mouse.

"This house is in pretty great shape," Mel said from behind her, slightly startling her friend.

"Hey, I was wondering when you'd spring to life!" she said, pushing her glasses into focus. "I was trying to do quiet jobs around here. It's too wet outside to plant. Tristan picked up some of the big branches before heading out to check for storm damage at his job sites. He put the branches on the flagstone patio so we can use them in the fireplace."

"What does Tristan do for a living?"

"He's a carpenter, I guess. He knows a lot of building stuff, and he helps out a lot around here. He actually supervises jobs for a big contractor. He also supervises me in the correct way of fixing things."

"He's a nice looking guy, nice personality . . . just a friend, huh?"

"Yes, he is just a friend. He rents a room and his mother was a friend of mine. How about I give you the grand tour of this house? It's only fifty cents!" Karen put down the spackle knife with a grin and led her off to present the house.

"This is the parlor with chestnut floors, a working fireplace, and seven huge windows. They overlook the front porch area. The wallpaper is true reproduction paper, silkscreened in San Francisco."

"Your furniture looks great in here, like it was meant for this room," Mel commented, remembering the little cottage that Karen used to have. That was the last time Mel had been home. Danny, Karen's husband, was still alive and they were only discussing moving.

"You've seen the banister. It's mostly chestnut. I have to remove some paint from the steps and bring it back to the original look. Every baluster is carved a little differently, making each unique. Under the steps over there is another little bathroom." They headed out the front door onto a vast flagstone porch.

They continued the tour of the Second Empire styled house, with its mansard slate roofline and intricate detailing of corbels and gables on the outside. The lady showed a full wear of many years of paint and details in shades of burgundy, greens, and tans. Some of the windows were still covered with original storms, still protecting wavy mature-glass windows. A very large flagstone patio flanked one side of the house just off the dining room. A pebble sidewalk ran around the perimeter of the house and into the gardens. An old gazebo that had seen better days held a small fountain. The gazebo flanked the side opposite from the large patio. The property housed several outbuildings, which included a barn, a shed, and a carriage house that now served as a two-car garage.

The magnificence of the dining room was in the burgundy and gold apple blossom paper. The ceiling boasted four layers of matching trims bordering the decadent cupid chandelier. Four large windows dressed in burgundy tapestry drapes, complete with gold fringe and tassels, guarded the window seats that were dressed in the same matching fabric. These windows overlooked the rolling greens to the east. A little oval-shaped stained glass window backlit a Rococo buffet piece. A little entrance foyer off to the west side hosted a great stained-glass window that allowed colored light to stream in. This little foyer room led to another door—a calling room.

Beyond the kitchen door just north of the dining area, walnut floors with original 1920s built-in cabinets flanked one half. A wall in the kitchen—original to the house—still had part of an old wood stove flue mounted in the wall. Thick pine bead boards flanked the walls to a chair rail height. Off to one side was yet another door to the outside and a small mud porch. A pantry door flanked the east side of the house where the washer and dryer were located. Off to the left corner was a back staircase that wound up to the second floor back room. Off the far end of the kitchen were living room quarters that had a built-in oak cabinet. The living room also boasted seven views of the back yard. Toward the end of the room a huge stained-glass bay was finished off with cozy bench seats. There was a knee wall with a marble top. An ornate gold tin ceiling outfitted this room, and an oversized door led to the rear of the house.

The second floor accommodated four bedrooms with detailed trim everywhere. The oblong bathroom resounded in a walnut finish. A romantic ball and claw tub sat as the centerpiece. A built-in walnut cabinet housed towels and personal items, and next to it was a heavy marble sink with large Gothic-shaped legs supporting it. Breaks of sunlight nibbled at the tub from sun dappling through antique lace curtains. The curtains graced two large windows that overlooked an iris garden in the side yard.

At the end of the bathroom, a different door led to another room whose three windows looked out upon the back and side yard. This room seemed to be an office, with the back stairs sneaking down into the kitchen area. Melissa was enchanted with her friend's beautiful home and was once again thankful she had made the trip back.

"I need to hook up with my brothers today. Hate to sleep and run on you, ol' pal. Wanna come with? I really miss them, and they are planning a big barbeque today. Glad the weather is working out for us. Look at that sunshine! Where can I store the stuff in my truck?"

"Gonna pass on this one; I plan to start stripping a piano stool that I picked up at an auction the other day. If it dries out some, I have some mums to get in the ground. You could take some of the boxes down to the basement and some to your room. I'll give you a hand. The basement is always dry. We're supposed to have more rain tomorrow as the Nor'easter rounds back from New England. I'm glad you are able to see your family today," Karen rambled as they unpacked Lissa's truck.

After unloading her truck, Mel spent the rest of the day in Jersey at her brother James's house in Cinnaminson. The day was damp but perfect for an old-fashioned barbeque. James had a nice deck that extended out of his two-story colonial.

It was grand to see her nieces and nephews. They had gotten so much bigger since she had last seen them at Christmas, but their personalities were the same. It was reassuring in a way, how family is a constant friend—always the same and yet ever changing.

❖

Chapter Three

Late Summer, 1920

He was just layering stone onto the final wall of an addition cellar that had been started earlier that spring. As soon as he had learned that a new baby was on the way, he started planning the addition. It took most of the summer, and he worked as late as the sun would allow. Now the cellar was almost finished, with hand-layered flat field stone for the walls. Field stones were easy to come by because farmers would just pile them at the end of a field of crops, such a nuisance they were. The lumber would be here next week to start framing the walls. The trees to be used as rafters were already split and drying.

He heard a crash of china and a scream through the open windows. Dropping the rock, he flew up the wooden ladder into the house. He found his wife sitting on the edge of a dining room chair, china bits all around her feet. His first thought was that she had cut herself. "Are you okay?" he asked, wiping his hand on his trousers before reaching for her pale hand. "What happened?"

"Call for the doctor, quick," she said in a frail, faint voice. The color had completely drained from her face. "I think it's the baby," she said, clutching her belly.

He ran to the parlor and wound up the phone, summoning the doctor. His hands shook with fear with the thought of losing another little one. The doctor told him to get his wife into bed. He was on his way.

Many hours passed as the midsummer sun faded into the music of cicadas humming in the trees. He paced for what seemed like several hours, then sat for another, then paced again. His nails were all chewed down now at the fear of losing his beloved Abbey—or another baby. He could only think of Abbey's attractive face, the glow that she possessed when pregnant. A new family member that would soon be upon them. The house was getting crowded with the live-in servant, his daughter Shirley, his son Victor, and his sister Adele, who stayed often. He was thankful that his sister had taken the children for a ride in her new car down to the city for a day of shopping. It made them so happy to be with Auntie Adele. They should be arriving home soon. What time is it? he thought. The sun was headed down to rest.

Dear Abbey, he thought, my beautiful wife of twelve years. He paced at the landing of the steps, back and forth from vestibule to parlor, occasionally sitting on the edge of Abbey's mother's cedar chest, which rested in the vestibule.

The doctor's wife came out of their bedroom to the landing. "Sam, could you come up? The doctor is just finishing up, and we'd like to talk to you."

As he got closer to the doctor's wife, she looked squarely at him and spoke softly. "Abbey is fine, but I'm sorry to say that your new son did not make it," she murmured, wiping her hands dry. "We did all we could to calm the contractions down, but it was just too early for him. She needs to be with you right now, and she needs several days of rest, but she will be fine."

Sam and his family buried the tiny casket with his son up on the hill next to Sam's parents. It was the hardest thing that he had ever done. It was the saddest day he and Abbey had ever experienced.

This baby, who was named Adam, was so close to life. So many tears were shed that day by all of the family, including his housekeeper. The addition to the house was painfully, temporarily forgotten as Sam busied himself with other work. He began to pour a lot of hours into his restaurant down on Main Street.

Chapter Four

Late Summer, 1920

S am's restaurant was known for the best pork barbecue around, with sweet cornbread, creamy coleslaw, and cold sweet tea. It was also known for Southern-style beans and rice and the best roasted chicken in the area. City folk stopped on their way up to Allentown, the Poconos, or to the State Park. Since the war ended, business at the restaurant had doubled. People were traveling more, and it seemed like everyone had something to drive as the automobiles became more popular. The restaurant also offered a few rooms for the overnight traveler when needed, but he wasn't in the hotel business.

Sam's place was doing fine. He had just finished painting the dining room and added some new gingham curtains and matching tablecloths. It was an idea that Lily, the doctor's wife, had suggested to keep Abbey's mind busy and off the loss of little Adam. It seemed to work for him and for her, too. She was happy again and sewing up a storm of fresh gingham.

Sam decided it was time to finish his other project. He needed to finish that addition. He really didn't need any extra rooms now that the baby was gone. He accepted his family and that was that. His parents had passed on last year, and now Abbey wouldn't be able to carry any more children. It was time to get on with life. The ground was starting to thaw from the winter, and spring was bringing new life to the landscape. The groundhog hadn't seen his shadow, so spring would be here soon.

The next day, Sam grabbed some help from town and began trimming the rafter trees that had sat all winter under canvas. He set to making cross timbers for the floor of the room. Usually houses were built using a twelve- to eighteen-inch space between rafters to support the floor boards on the first floor. Sam butted the logs tightly together, using wire to hold them in place. When this was done, he wrapped tar paper over the top of the logs and sealed it with hot tar. His basement was now waterproof, but an unattractive appendage to his beautiful Second Empire home. He had an idea in mind to cover the top of this ugly extra basement.

The next week, he brought in some flat slate from a quarry upstate and created a beautiful patio for his Abbey. It was completed with white wrought-iron patio furniture and planters that his sister Adele and Abbey had purchased at Lit Brothers Department Store in the city. Abbey was already searching bulb catalogs for late spring blooms to go around the perimeter of the patio. Life was getting back to normal, and he was glad.

Adele and Abbey sat having iced tea on a cool sunny afternoon. They had just finished putting in bulbs for late spring with the help of a boy from town.

Adele said, "Did you read about the uproar the Volstead Act has caused? Crime in the big cities is up because of prohibition. Senator Volstead wants to create a new police force to control it."

"I just don't see how they can listen to a bunch of bible-banging, drum-playing, and ugly temperance women and create such a law! When the New Year rang in, the shock of it was felt when six people in town were arrested for selling and drinking alcohol past twelve o'clock. That Senator Volstead should be run out of Washington," Abbey protested to her sister-in-law, brushing invisible crumbs from her apron. "You just can't take away people's rights like that."

"Well, there is talk of a new police group being organized to stop these new speakeasies from starting up. Now who will pay for that?"

"I know. I heard it on the radio show the other day. Congress wants a separate agency to watchdog the distillers and mobs. I mean, what is this world coming to? I know more people drinking now than before the new law started in January." She paused. "Funny, how it was legal to drink one minute and against the law the next."

"I just don't know, Abbey. There are so many new conveniences and ideas, but not a drop to celebrate with. It just isn't right. I feel sorry for those who served in the war. Some of them need a way to forget the blood."

Speaking slowly and cautiously, Abbey placed her hand on Adele's leg and said, "Adele, if I tell you something, you must keep it in the strictest confidence."

"Of . . . of course, Abbey!" Adele said, placing her hand on Abbey's.

"Your brother is thinking of making a still in our basement. He said he has all of the ingredients at the restaurant to start one. The sugar, corn meal. . . . He just needs to build a tank in which to brew the concoction."

"Does he have someone to sell it to?"

"Have you ever met that cute butcher that delivers pork to Sam from South Philadelphia? He has asked Sam almost every month since this law began last year. He said Sam is perfect to start up a still because we are isolated out here and we already have the key ingredients. He would deliver it to the right people in the city."

"Does he need our help? We could start collecting jars and ketchup bottles. I'm with the two of you—whatever you decide. This law is the worst our government has ever come up with. Why, I just heard of a speakeasy going in at the famous Mayfair Inn and another in Lower Black Eddy."

"I don't understand how they can be so blatant to open up these speakeasies. Have you ever been to one?"

"Actually, some of my girlfriends and I went shopping for the new style dresses and shoes and we even put a feather in our hair! We piled into my Buick and went there like school girls. It was so much fun. We had to pay at the door, which allowed us to drink for free. So technically we weren't buying liquor. The music was great! I even learned that new dance all of the young people are doing, the Charleston!" Adele said, sitting up properly and pushing her skirt over her knee. "It was quite decadent and lots and lots of fun," she said, waving both her hands, palms open, in a flapper dance gesture.

"How exciting!" Abbey exclaimed, bringing her hand to rest over her chest. "I wish I could see some of the excitement. Can you show me the dance steps? The most I've done is this short bob of hair, which I adore. It is so easy to manage. My hair dries so much faster now."

"It looks great on you with your natural curls! So trendy and youthful with the new look. You are just as daring as my brother. I am worried about Sam getting in trouble with the still, though."

"I'm worried, too, Adele. We could lose everything, but. . . ." Abbey paused, putting her hand under her bob of hair. She was still not used to the shortness of it, but liked how it felt. "I trust and love Sam, and he has never let us down, so I will stick by him. He wants to save the money for our children so that they can get an education and not fight in a war like he had to."

❖

Chapter Five

Present Day

Sunday morning brought more clouds with the threat of the Nor'easter heading back down from New England. Lissa showered and dressed early and met up with Trist in the kitchen for coffee.

"Mornin', Lissa," Tristan said, handing her a mug. "Cream is on the counter. What are your plans for today?" His hand had touched hers and he thought, how nice.

"I'm not sure. Where is Karen?" she said, putting a spoonful of sugar in the mug.

"She went to an early Mass; she'll be back by nine."

"What are you doing today?"

"I dunno; maybe go to the Shoprite and pick up some ingredients for a huge tray of lasagna. It isn't very exciting."

"Well, do you mind if I tag along with you? It looks like a long day of rain. I could pick up a few things, and if you drove, I could check out new things in this area. Get a feel for the roads again."

They left a note for Karen and headed out. Tristan showed Lissa the "Village Proper" just a few miles up the main road from Karen's house. She could see several new homes being developed on the roads leading to the downtown area. The village retained its old-fashioned charm. It held a few gift shops, an ice cream parlor, a liquor store, and post office, but it was lacking a good restaurant. Several buildings were unoccupied. A few larger homes on the edge of town had been converted to professional offices. One building stood out to Lissa. It was a three-story brick-front building with a cornice trim at the top. The brickwork was fancy around the windows with a keystone over each window. "That's a traditional Philadelphia design," she told Tristan. The building looked empty. The windows were whitewashed, making the building look arctic, but for some reason it warmed her heart.

Tristan was so excited to have Lissa with him. She had just jumped into his truck like she did it every day. What was it with this girl? She even sported a baseball cap and ponytail, and he thought that was so sexy. He just hoped he wasn't boring her. The conversations with her seemed endless and always exciting. He felt that maybe they had crossed paths once or twice. They had attended the same concerts, danced at the same night clubs out of high school, and even swam in the same lake when they were kids. He thought about her as she pointed out different building styles in town. He had never met a girl who impressed him more.

They headed back through town, south down Route 32, along the Delaware River. Flooding was evident in low-lying backyards. The water was murky and fast-moving. The radio said that the river was expected to crest at noontime, but it could get higher if the storm stalled over the area.

They pulled into the market and Lissa grabbed a cart. They almost filled the cart with cheeses, bread, spinach, garlic, and some cold cuts for lunch. Lissa offered to pay for half the groceries, but Tristan said no. They loaded the groceries into a compartment behind the seats and headed back up Route 32.

Lissa liked this guy, who knew about food and fooled around with fruit in the produce aisle. He even started to jokingly flirt with a few of the melons. He looked great in a tee shirt, torn jeans, and a zippered hoodie. She purposely touched his arm while handing him the bags of food. Was she beginning to fall for him?

Past experiences had told her not to get crazy right away. Hunger and desire had a way of controlling a bad relationship. Take your time, she cautioned herself. Take your time and don't scare him away. There is no need to rush. She liked him mainly because he was kind, he listened to what she had to say, and he didn't cut her off in mid-sentence like so many men in the past had—all those self-centered creeps who had wasted her time. She actually had decided to quit dating for a while.

They were back along the river when Lissa looked to the right and noticed a dog running back and forth on a piece of land. The size of the land was no larger than the size of a small garage. The flooding had formed an island where there used to be a high spot on the river's edge. "Stop the truck!" she commanded, placing her hand on the dashboard in preparation.

Tristan quickly slowed to a stop, looking all over. "What? What is it?"

"Look!" She jumped out of the truck and headed down to the river's edge.

Tristan caught up with her. There on the island of land was a muddy Irish setter. He had a collar with a broken and dangling leash. "I wonder how he got out there. We need to get him back here soon. If the water crests in a few hours, that piece of land will disappear." He turned and headed back up the hill to grab some rope from the back of his truck.

"What are you going to do?" Lissa said, helping him undo the rope.

"Well," he paused briefly, putting a plan in his head. "I'm going to tie this to my waist and wade across the water to the dog. It doesn't look that deep, but tie this to a tree in case the current is too strong for me." He stopped and looked Lissa in the eyes. Her pretty face had a scrunched brow. "Don't worry; I'll be okay. I do this all the time!" He smiled and touched her cheek with his warm hand.

She tied the other end of the rope to a tree, and he started to head into the water. "Wait!" she screamed. "Your cell phone and wallet, please!"

"Why, I hardly know you," he smirked. He handed her his hoodie, thinking that it might weigh him down. The water was moving very fast. The river smelled of musk and danger. It was very cold, even though the air was relatively warm and muggy.

She felt a rush inside her. Adrenalin, she wondered, or something else? Her heart pounded. I should call 911—they should be notified, she thought. "Be careful, it might be slippery!" she yelled as she punched in the numbers.

She called the authorities while he slowly waded in, getting a feel for the uneven, grassy, muddy floor. She had to estimate where they were, since there were no landmarks near them. This irritated the 911 dispatcher. Tristan was about halfway now, and the current looked like it was coming faster. It had pushed him downstream from his initial launch site. She held tightly to the rope, slowly feeding tautness. The water had a musky scent of stagnant pond and fresh-turned mud. The rain was brief, which usually happens when a Nor'easter turns back; the powerful clouds seem to break apart. Storms broken down can wreak havoc in one area and leave another perfectly sunny.

He made it across and climbed onto the grassy, slippery island. The frightened dog kept barking at him, an intruder on his small piece of territory. Tristan held out his hand and talked very softly to him. The barking slowly stopped and the frightened setter started to sniff him. Tristan was able to check his collar. It read "Penny." "Okay, Penny, it will be okay," he repeated several times to her. Penny tilted her head and started to lick his face. A shiver ran through his body, bringing him back to the situation.

A large tree branch floated by and snagged Tristan's rope and then let it go, which pulled him off balance a little. He was covered in mud. This was enough for him to see the danger he could be in if the water raised any faster. He had lived here long enough to know that all of the tributaries and storm drains emptied into the Delaware. This often created a problem for riverside properties near Trenton, Flemington, and further south.

He looked up the river. There was another large tree or branch headed his way, but he thought it might snag a few times or bypass the little part that he had to cross. He cuddled up to Penny, talking to her so she would stay calm. He explained that they were going to cross over the water but she could have all of his cold cuts if she stayed still and calm. Like most women he met, she was charmed by his voice, and he held her tight as they moved back into the water. It seemed a few inches higher in the waist and a few degrees colder.

Lissa held the back of her hand to her face, she was so afraid. Where were the police or fire department? She started pulling the rope to tighten the tension. She looked up the river and noticed a large tree floating Tristan's way. She tried not to show fear, but inside a little voice was saying, "Hurry, hurry, hurry!"

He was about halfway across now. "It isn't far," he softy assured the dog and himself.

Penny remained calm and trusting. The weight of this dog and the chill of the water was sinking into his bones and exhausting him. He tried to stay focused on the land, watching Lissa. Focus. He could make it. He was only twenty feet away now. He should be touching land soon.

Just as he approached the edge, a branch raced into the section behind him. He thought it had missed him. Suddenly the branch swirled round and clipped him on the arm. He held tightly to Penny and kept going. As soon as he was on the grass, he let go of her. Lissa, still keeping the rope taut, came and helped him up out of harm's way. Penny was excitedly barking her thanks. Lissa grabbed his slightly dry hoodie off the ground and wrapped it around his chilled body.

"You're hurt!" she wailed. "Look, blood!" She was rubbing his arms, trying to warm him up.

"It's just a scratch," he said, leaning in to her to steal the warmth from the sweatshirt and from her. He looked up and saw her look of worry. Just as she turned, he caught her lips and they kissed and then kissed again. His body warmed exponentially. He looked over her shoulder and saw a patrol car pulling over.

Lissa sighed deeply, her legs twitched inside, and a fire shot through her veins. She looked up at him, catching his gaze over her shoulder. She turned to see an officer getting out of his car. They both rose from their sitting positions at the edge of the water. Lissa explained the story to the officer while Tristan gave the promised reward to Penny. She ate it furiously.

"You must have been out there all night, huh, girl?" he cooed in a puppy language.

The officer said a family upriver was looking for a dog that had turned up missing that morning. The backyard was flooded where she stayed, and the family thought she might have drowned. Several minutes went by and a car stopped. Three young kids jumped out as Penny ran barking to them. All in a day's work, Tristan thought, glancing down at his muddy, soaking body. He looked over at Lissa, who was just staring at him, and the chill turned to warmth inside him.

They got back to the house to find Karen waiting for them. She looked at the muddy couple holding bags of groceries in her kitchen and was reminded of an old saying.

"Yup, that's another fine mess you've gotten us into, Lucy!" she quipped. "You got some 'splaining to do," she said in a light Hispanic accent, and they all giggled.

Tristan showered and dressed in sweats, then helped Melissa with dinner while Karen made a salad. After dinner the three close friends cuddled under a blanket on the sofa in front of an M. Night Shyamalan movie. He was a local man who had made it big.

❖

Chapter Six

Present Day

I t was 3:35 a.m. when she opened her eyes the first time. She closed them and tried to return to that cozy, forgiving haven of sleep. Her mind was racing as she closed her eyes again. The whitewashed building haunted her. At 4:00 a.m., she was up. She grabbed her robe, sweatpants, and laptop and headed down to the kitchen. She found a box of herbal tea and fired up the Internet on her computer.

She punched in the address of the building, 57 Main Street, Black Eddy, PA. One hundred search results came up. She really was only interested in the real estate sites. Two sites beckoned with information about the address in question. She found a tablet and started writing. Occasionally, she would stop and refer to the Internet. She searched for the history of the building. She searched the area's history. She was so into the jotting down and searching that she didn't hear Tristan come into the kitchen.

He was normally quiet so as not to wake Karen, so he was surprised to see the wild-haired brunette typing away at the laptop. He tiptoed in silently and said softly in her ear, "Hello, gorgeous."

She jumped, practically bumping her head into his chin. "Ah shit, man, you startled me!"

"I'm sorry to do that to you. What are you working on?"

"What are you doing scaring people in the middle of the night?"

"Lissa, its 5:30 a.m.! I usually hit The Lumber Depot by 6:15. Want some coffee?"

"Oh, sure. My tea is cold now, anyway. I couldn't sleep. Did you ever have one of those nights when an idea pops into your head and you just have to get up and do something with it?" she said, touching her face and hoping her makeup wasn't smeared.

"So, what keeps a beautiful hairdo like that up all night?" Tristan said with a crooked smirk.

"I'm so excited! Look, I found the realtor of the building on Main Street. I have a few ideas for names." She picked up the tablet and moved closer to him. He smelled delicious, she thought, trying to smooth down her hair with her free hand and hoping he hadn't noticed too much. "I jotted down themes, accountants, history, and suppliers. I finally have something that will tie me down to one place. Something I can call my own. I'm going to own my own restaurant!"

"Well, gorgeous, I will help you any way I can. We seem to make a great team, rescuing dogs and shopping. Why not a restaurant? I will help you in any way I can! Just let me know what I can do. I know we just met, but we seem to be hitting it off. Would you like to join me today? I have to check all of my jobs from the weather—drop off some supplies and install a few windows." It doesn't sound like much fun, Tristan thought after he had finished the invite.

"Sure," she exclaimed with a little more enthusiasm than she should have shown. I'm so not cool, she thought. Pace yourself, she admonished herself. "Sure, I just have to slip into some work clothes and I will be right back down."

Karen shuffled in. "Morning, Karen," Lissa said and gave her friend a big kiss on her way out of the kitchen. "What's on your agenda today?"

"I have a big meeting at work, and choir practice right after, so I won't be home till after eight o'clock tonight. You guys go ahead and eat without me. One of our choir members owns a pizza place and always brings food to church for us."

"Well, then, I better hurry up and get ready to go to job sites today. How exciting," she said with a big grin, moving her hand through her hair like a big five-pronged comb. She gave Karen a big hug and was off.

She ran into the shower and tossed on jeans, two tee shirts, and a zippered hoodie. She dug her work boots out of the suitcase. She tossed mousse in her hair, did her makeup in record speed and was down looking brilliant for Tristan in twenty minutes flat.

Karen was at the sink washing her cereal bowl. "Holy moly, you clean up fast." Karen giggled and looked over at Tristan, who had an impressive flat smile on his face. She was quite pleased with the unity of these two good friends. They were good people who needed a loving relationship, like she had enjoyed in her marriage with Danny.

Her body sagged when she thought of Danny's tragic hunting accident, her best friend and husband taken just when life was supposed to slow down for both of them.

Tristan looked at Karen and asked, "Is something wrong?"

"Oh, no! You two go to work and have fun. I just started thinking about Danny. I just miss him."

The day was terrific, and Melissa enjoyed every minute of Tristan's company. She met the different work crews. She made an effort to remember their names. She helped staple Tyvek to the frames before the windows went in and helped Tristan square the windows they installed. Some of the jobs were a little bit muddy, and at one point she actually slid down a muddy embankment of dirt and landed on her knee. Tristan had stretched out a big strong arm to pick her up. Then he reached for her face and wiped a little splatter of mud from her cheek. That had sent the warm juices flowing in her. They both made eye contact.

Tristan was amazed at her vitality and at his acceptance of this new girl in his life. Wow, he thought, she is so beautiful and uncomplicated. She even got along with miserable ol' José, who complains about everything. Mel and José inspected a draft of studs leading to the deck for the walls on the first job. Then José showed her how to cut headers in preparation for the next day. I need to take her out tonight for a really nice dinner—very girly, he thought.

As the day came to an end, Melissa found herself very happy, a little chilled, and very satisfied from working outside. Her adrenaline or something was fueling her energy, in spite of the lack of sleep. She was covered with dirt and clay from lifting studs to the deck with José. She had made a bet with him that she could move as much as he could. Now he owed her a cold beer. Tristan got off the phone and approached her as she sat on his tailgate, wiping off her hands.

"Hey, gorgeous, how about I take you out for a really nice dinner?"

"Maybe we could get cleaned up first. Do you know any pubs that serve black and tans and really great burgers?"

"Yup," he smiled. "It's a plan, then."

❖

Chapter Seven

Summer, 1921

S am opened up his restaurant at the same time every day. He was a man of routine for the most part. It was eight in the morning and the sun was already bright in the sky. He opened up the windows and cranked on the belt-driven ceiling fans. The restaurant was looking very fine these days, and it was doing quite well. They were in full travel season now, so lots of days, travelers were in town from Philadelphia and New York. They all stopped at Sam's Smokey BBQ Restaurant, 57 Main Street in Black Eddy on the way to the Ringing Rocks State Park, just up the road from the restaurant. The park had unusual rock formations that actually rang and many caves for kids to explore in.

He fired up the big kettle to make sweet tea and opened the back door for the ice delivery. He still had an old cedar walk-in ice box. The ice blocks were hoisted up to the top of the box daily to keep them cold. The water would drain down a rubber hose to the alley. He was already shopping around for a new compressor type. He went out to the smoke cabinet thirty feet in the yard and started piling in the lumber in preparation for another smoke. He usually smoked meat every other day during the high season and less in the winter. He looked up from his hickory pile to see Jake pulling into the yard.

"Hey, Jake, how's it going today?" He gave the man a short hand wave.

"Well, it took forever to pick up the ice blocks with my truck this morning, and the wife and kids had me up late last night. They want to go down to Cape May for the weekend. My wife is always planning ways to spend my side money. I should get them out of the city once in awhile, though. She has had them to the zoo a few times, and picnics out at Fairmount Park. They usually go to the neighborhood park or play stick ball in the street."

"Well, that sounds like a nice break for you, also. Do you want to borrow my car to get down there?" Sam said as he started helping unload the wooden boxes of pork loins into the smoke shed.

Some time later, Jake started moving the wooden crates back into the truck. They were now filled with bottles of Sam's fine bourbon whiskey, neatly wrapped in the butcher paper that Jake had provided for him. The butcher paper made it look like boxes of pork, just in case he was ever stopped. A real friendship had been struck as they ventured into this extra and illegal trade. When Jake got back to the city, he would stop and make his final delivery to a warehouse on Front Street. They paid him well, and Sam got his weekly cut. Jake's boss at the pork house was none the wiser and didn't miss the dozen crates or so that Jake had lifted. The mob guys provided them with all of the bottles that they needed, and often replenished them by recycling the bottles at the speakeasy level. Jake had read in the *Philadelphia Bulletin* about a truckload of bottles that had been hijacked on the way to the tomato juice factory in Camden. He often wondered if these were the same bottles that they were using to fill with the golden liquor.

Jake and Sam arranged for the pick-up of his car. His wife would get a babysitter and they would come up Friday after work to pick up the car for the weekend, leaving Sam the pork truck to drive.

Sam's still was in full swing at the house, and had become a part of his weekly routine. He would wait until dark at the restaurant to put sacks of sugar and cornmeal in his trunk. The rest was easy. It had taken no time at all to construct the copper still. The rubber hoses were also easy to come by, and as the mash fermented, the pure bourbon flowed from the tubes. As a young kid before the war, he had learned from his friend's grandfather how to make smooth Kentucky bourbon. Unlike Sam, the old man would run his water through burned wood to give it that smoky taste similar to Jack Daniel's whiskey. The grandfather often let the boys have a swig. This made for several lazy, hazy afternoons beside his grandfather's pond.

The smell was a challenge. It took Sam a long time to figure out how to engineer the odor. His still was in the basement of his house. How would he keep the sour twang out of the living area? He lined the basement walls with tar and tar paper. He painted the walls white. The first step was to provide a flame retardant in case of fire, and the white color to allow him to see well. He hoped to contain the smell to two vents. He dug a long trench across the yard and filled it with galvanized pipe. He placed two small trees at the sight of the venting to mark the spot and keep lawn tractors away. He then placed a screen over the hole so that small animals wouldn't get in and nest. He made a rock circle so the average person would think it was a fire pit or abandoned well. Inside the room, he placed two black cast iron fans on a shelf near the vent holes and left them running all of the time.

Jake was a tremendous help in the delivery and setting up of the business arrangement. He originally met his contact at one of the Italian restaurants that he delivered to. It wasn't long after that they had arranged the pork box exchange. Due to the time of year, it was easy to go undetected, as there were not many people around in the early spring.

Sam's restaurant was a perfect foil, as he was already buying the main ingredients. The *Philadelphia Bulletin* had written stories of people being snagged by purchasing large quantities of sugar. In the last few months, the Feds were getting more aggressive, and more officers, referred to as "G-Men," were being hired to police the prohibited alcohol industry. Sam had slowly doubled his normal buying list, and he was hoping to go undetected.

Sam was now producing thirty to fifty gallons of fine Philadelphia-style bourbon each week. He took great pride in distilling his liquid gold. He had three fifty-gallon oak barrels in the corner of the basement that the condensing coil dripped into. Inside the oak barrels were dozens of burned apricots and apples, to give the bourbon a sweet smoky taste. This was a similar idea to the burnt wood that his friend's grandfather used to use in his bourbon. This was Abbey's idea. She said, "If you are going to make something, then make it good." She also thought that smoking the fruit would help keep the sour smell out of the house.

The bourbon would sit for seven days in the barrel, so Sam would work from the barrel distilled the week before. Each night he would spend two to three hours in the basement bottling or starting a new mash. Some nights Abbey would join him in the bottling process. She didn't mind the still and accommodated her house for it. She had an old bottle stopper machine that her father had given her. He had used it to put up ketchup, but it worked very nicely for pushing the corks into the bottles of bourbon. It was a relaxing job for Abbey. She enjoyed these evenings alone with her husband. They had gotten into the routine of working, and they were able to chat about things other than the normal business and household events. She sometimes sat and watched Sam fill the bottles. She loved him so much.

Chapter Eight

Summer, 1922

S am opened the restaurant at 8:00 a.m. as usual and put the kettle on for fresh sweet tea. He had added honey to the list of ingredients needed to complete his hooch operation. A local farmer provided him with an adequate supply in exchange for a small bottle of liquor. They documented some of the honey transactions since the G-Men were getting more and more vigilant. Sam started adding honey to his sweet tea just in case he was ever audited. This didn't bother Sam much. He was just a small-time bootlegger, as he felt he should be called after making his golden booze for a year now. He always ordered the same ingredients, worked the same hours, and had even built a nice friendship with Jake, the driver. Life was going well with no complications . . . until noon that day.

Sam had hired on two waitresses to help him with lunch, and occasionally Abbey would come down and help him with the cooking. She had a slightly used car to drive on her own now. Sam and Adele had taken her out for lessons, and she absolutely loved driving. She always offered to pick up ingredients for Sam or run errands—anything she could do to get behind the wheel of freedom.

The small bell on the door tingled, announcing another customer. Sally, one of his wait staff, came back to tell Sam that someone was interested in renting a room. She added that he wasn't a local and rolled her big grey-blue eyes. Sam washed his hands from pulling pork and came out to the counter.

A short man standing just five-feet-two inches tall stood with his back against the wall, analyzing the rest of the patrons in the place. He had a small oval face, round glasses, and a pasty complexion. His thinning hair was combed back and plastered with some hair grease. He was holding his hat, which he promptly put on the counter. He was dressed in a black suit with a faded black shirt and black tie. Sam thought that with his hat on, this little man probably looked like a Scaramouch, an Italian clown known for his dark outfit and disloyal ways. It came from a book that he had picked up in the war while stationed in Italy.

The man spoke in a slight voice, "The post office told me that you have rooms to rent."

"Yes. How long might you be staying?" Sam asked as he grabbed the clipboard with the room rental form on it.

"I'm not sure yet," the little man replied. "It could be a week or two weeks. I have business here, and I am not sure how long it will take." He picked at the brim of the hat that he held.

"What kind of business are you in?" Sam inquired in a friendly gesture.

"Well," the man said, "I work for the federal government. That is all I can say for now." He wiped the corners of his mouth. He was brief and to the point. He exerted very little energy to speak and never looked directly at Sam.

In the back of his mind, Sam thought, They are hiring anyone to search out bootleggers. Sam always knew this day would come, but meeting this guy didn't frighten him as he had thought it might. The man was like a little bug in his mind's eye.

Sam said, "Well, let me know how I can help you. Our rooms have a private door from the restaurant. We clean every Thursday. You will have a hot plate for coffee and some fixings for that in your room. I don't serve breakfast, but I am open for lunch and dinner, and if you want you can purchase extra cornbread and honey for breakfast. We make the best!"

Sam led the little man outside to show him to the room upstairs. "Where do you hail from, and what is your name?" Sam asked.

"I'm from Alexandria, Virginia, originally. I came in from Philadelphia this morning from our field office there. My name is Dick Shutter," he said with a noticeable twang this time. He used one hand to wipe the corners of his mouth again and held his hat with the other.

"Well, here we are. My name is Sam Rhoades. You'll find the linens fresh once a week. If you need anything, stop in down the stairs. We open at eleven o'clock daily for lunch. The best sweet tea and pulled pork this far north."

"Thank you," the Scaramouch said with his small voice as he wiped the corners of his mouth yet again.

❖

Chapter Nine

Present Day

M el sat at the edge of the bed for a moment. It was 6:30, and she was fully dressed in her construction garb of jeans and boots. Her tops were two tee shirts with a jean shirt over top, and a hoodie sat beside her. She knew what she had to do, but how was this going to affect her relationship with Tristan? They had really bonded these past few weeks.

The night before, she had a girls-on-the-edge-of-the-bed conversation with Karen, her ol' sock, her ol' kid, her ol' pal. Karen, who loved her and loved Tristan also, helped her see the light. Karen was right in her judgment of Melissa. Lissa had often since high school become the chameleon—changing her colors when she met a new man. She had even done it with Karen by trying to join Karen's choir in high school. Melissa didn't have an ounce of music or voice to give to the choir. So, as Karen pointed out, she was doing it once again by following the life and times of Tristan and ignoring her own true love—cooking. Karen also pointed out that maybe this was why she and José often sat at lunch swapping recipes and cooking secrets.

Melissa knew that today would be her last day hanging out at the construction sites, even though she enjoyed doing so. Today they were going to have the crane on site to lift the trusses into place. This meant that there wouldn't be much for her to do, but it would be exciting to watch. Tristan would have two to four guys on the rim to catch the crane's trusses and place them in. The other two guys would be nailing them in. He didn't want her up high on the rafters, so she was in charge of stapling insulating wrap on the house and around the windows. This was okay for her, and she was excited to watch the whole process.

In addition, today José was bringing a special meatball rolled in mashed potatoes and bread crumbs and then fried. He was also bringing a piece of blood sausage that he had purchased especially for her to try. She didn't want to let her buddy José down.

❖

Chapter Ten

Present Day

On the way home that evening, Mel asked if they could stop and have a beer before going up to the house. She knew Tristan was a little tired from pushing trusses all day, but maybe this would relax him and help prepare her for what she had to tell him. They stopped at their favorite pub at the edge of Black Eddy, a small place that may have been a gas station at one time in its life.

When the first round was poured and served, Melissa spoke. "Tristan, you know I've had a great time with you on your jobs. I've learned so much."

"Well, we've enjoyed having you," Tristan said. He swiped his hand across the top of his lip, trying not to show a beer mustache. "You did a great job today and every day. We love having you, especially the old grouch."

"Don't call my buddy José an old grouch! The thing is I need to smell garlic, have my eyes burn from peeling onions, flip something in a frying pan, and yell for waitresses."

"So you wanna cook dinner for me?" Tristan said with a sly grin. "Where will we get the waitresses?"

Frowning and keeping her eyes focused on her beer, Lissa said, "I called a chef friend of mine. Turns out he's desperate, and he needs some help fast. His sous chef, John, hurt his back deep-sea fishing last week. It sounded pretty bad—he slipped when a big wave hit the boat and bent his back across the bow. I'm going to help him tomorrow."

As soon as she finished, she felt better, as if weights had been lifted from her shoulders. Gee, I must really like this guy to care this much about how he feels, she thought.

"Listen, Mel. I never expected you to give up what you do and love, but I do thank you for spending time in my work life. I've never met anyone that did that for me before."

As he spoke, he put his hand on hers. Her hand was cool, and his was warm.

Mel was surprised by the heat of his hand touching hers. She thought her hand must feel like it belonged to an ice queen. She also thought that maybe it was time to take their relationship to the next level. This was another subject that she had discussed with Karen. Her house, her rules, her friends, and Mel didn't want to offend her friend. Trist and she had been inseparable for more than two weeks now. The few rounds of kissing had ended up pretty close, but they both seemed to hold back. She wondered if he sensed her hesitation. Yeah, he probably did think she was an ice queen. Most of the girls she had worked with in the past would take a guy in one night.

"So what time should I expect you in the kitchen tomorrow?" she said with a smirk and moved her hand down to touch his knee. She looked into his big light blue eyes and smiled widely. "Karen has choir tonight."

Understanding the message immediately, he called, "Bartender!" and quickly paid the tab.

❖

Chapter Eleven

Present Day

They entered the house holding hands. As soon as they reached the second floor, they were kissing, touching, exploring, and un-buttoning. They pulled layers of tee shirts and sweatshirts off one another.

Holding her hand, Tristan said, "Follow me," and he led her into the bathroom and started a shower.

She got extra towels out. They barely stopped touching each other, afraid to break the moment.

"Is this okay with you if we shower? I am so dirty from work, but I don't want to let go of you for now."

"Absolutely," she said, and she started to caress his firm bare chest, which had the perfect amount of chest hair.

He helped her finish with her bra and panties, caressing every female part. "I hope the hot water doesn't run out before we get wet," Tristan said with a smirk. He nibbled at her full breasts, and she gently pulled him into the flowing, hot shower.

The rest of the night was more than they had expected. Every move, every touch completed a divine desire that had been building since that first night of the storm. Although they were both physically tired from a day of construction, their desire was in overdrive with plenty of fuel to burn.

That night, Tristan told Lissa that he admired and cared about her. He told her over and over how beautiful she was. It sent shivers down her body. He said it wasn't something that he came by saying very easily, but he thought he was in love with her. He said he knew it within the first few days, and he had confirmed it by waiting to make love to her. He wanted their first time together to be special and long lasting. He told her all of the qualities that he adored about her. He loved her hair and her independence. The way she made everyone she met feel special.

Lissa too, expressed her admiration for Tristan. She said she knew there was an attraction the day he rescued the dog from the island. She said she just needed to add a few more spices to the stew, and keep him simmering, before she knew for sure that he would be delicious. As she said this, she licked his chest all the way up to his lips, and they both shuddered. They were a perfect fit together and held and kissed each other for a very long time.

They talked, touched, caressed, and explored each other until about two in the morning, when sleep overtook their desire. They awoke at the crack of dawn, feeling comfortable with each other, and touched, hugged, and made love again.

❖

Chapter Twelve

Abbey, 1922

She was enjoying life. Her children were healthy, beautiful, and sweet. Her husband loved her more than he ever had. Life was good. She embraced the changes that kept coming her way with new ambition or challenge and left the fear behind. It was an empowering time for women, and she was up for the challenge. The opportunities for women were growing daily.

It was exciting to vote. People, even men, wanted to know what she was thinking. She loved learning to drive and experiencing the freedom it made her feel. She had new clothes and shoes and a daring new haircut. A new vacuum cleaner, washer, phone, and refrigerator to help with her household chores—yes, oh yes, this decade was starting off beautifully! She felt strong and incredibly happy with her life.

She awoke that morning and decided that the slight tang in the air caused by the brewing in the extended cellar was getting to her. She started to bake more pies and cakes for Sam down at the restaurant. She browned off some apricots for his next brew. This hid some of the smell, and it was really only strong in the kitchen and dining room. The rest of the house was fine for the most part, but some days the smell drifted stronger. Still, the fall was approaching, and windows would be closing soon. She pondered about another way of hiding the scent.

The previous week, while making some cherry pies and candles for the house, the idea had hit her. She took some of the hot candle wax and added spices to it that were sitting on the counter from the pie. She took nutmeg, cinnamon, and ginger and added it to the wax. Once it was set, she lit her experiment. She loved it! It seemed to hide any sour smell and filled the nostrils and room with a delicious scent. Today, she would take action on this idea.

She went down to the Kresgie Five and Dime Store, in her own car, with her own egg money, and purchased two cases of canning jars, wax wicks, perfume, spices, mint oil, rose oil, lemon oil, and other interesting possibilities. She went home thinking of a million potential concoctions for her candles. Move over, Sam, she thought to herself, I can brew, too! She felt alive and happy—more than she had felt in years.

Once home, she went up to Sam's closet and put on a shirt of his and a pair of his trousers. How nice and comfortable this was. She pinned her bob back with a hankie and flew back down to the kitchen with vigor and empowerment. The chandelier-dusting that she had planned for the day would have to wait. She was excited about her new project!

Her mama had taught her how to make all types of candles: stick, tapered, jar, and votive, and she had molds for most of them. "Best to have plenty of candles on hand, dear," her mama used to say. This was before electricity was so plentiful and steady. She and Mama would make candles twice a month, then less once electricity started to get more regular. Mama used to say that candles would never go out of style because of the life they gave to a room. She wondered why Mama had never mixed coconut oil and cinnamon into her wax.

❖

Chapter Thirteen

Sam and Abbey, 1922

He stood by the back door of the kitchen watching the women busy at the counter. His heart fluttered at her appearance. She was stunning. She was humming a new popular song. Her hair was pushed back and covered with a scarf. She wore his pants and shirt. Clothes had never looked better on her. He noticed every curve. She hadn't heard him enter as she flitted around setting wicks in candles. He slowly crept up behind her and put his arm around her waist, startling Abbey from her intense concentration.

"Hello, you beautiful woman; have you seen my wife around?"

"Well, no, I haven't—big, strong, and handsome! I could fill in for her if you like," she said, smirking, lowering a pot of wax chunks onto a double boiler. She turned to him and planted a big smooch on his lips.

His loins jumped with excitement. Who was this new creature standing in front of him? He started to kiss her neck and pulled the scarf off of her bundled head. Short sexy hair, tiny waist bound in those very becoming pants. I haven't been taking enough care of this fantastic creature living with me, he thought. His hands slowly glided down her waist.

"What's for dinner?" he asked, and she replied, "You!" She clicked off the gas stove and pushed him toward the back staircase. "No one is home but us."

They started kissing like they had when they were courting so many years before. Thank you, Adele, for taking the kids to Cape May for the weekend, Abbey thought. Sam and Abbey did everything that they would usually forego with children and a housekeeper at home. They even filled the big ball and claw tub and bathed together. That evening took their relationship as man and wife to another level. They certainly loved each other.

Later on, while lying in bed, Sam said, "You plumb wore me out, woman. I'm starved, and I still have to work an hour in the basement."

"Well," she said, "I guess I will release you from my spell for a few hours. Hope your wife doesn't show up!" She smiled happily. "If you come back to me later, I'll throw you a sandwich to keep you going." She took his hand and rubbed it across her flat belly, stopping at her triangle patch of fur.

They dressed and went back to their work. Later, when Abbey had finished her last batch of wax and was all cleaned up, Sam came into the kitchen, where she sat at the table labeling her scented collection.

"What's all of this?" he said.

"I thought that I might rent the little office next door to the restaurant and start selling candles to tourists. Here, smell some of them." She held a cinnamon-coconut combination to his nose. "I started doing the candles as a way of getting the mash smell down, especially with the fall approaching, but why not make money at it as well?"

"The candles smell good enough to eat, I'm so hungry. And I love the idea, Abbey, but who will you get to run it?"

"I don't know, maybe a few moms in town looking to sell other things that they make. Donna Smith, the sheriff's wife, crochets potholders. Sally puts ribbons on the edge of towels, and Kelliann puts up amazing jams. I could find lots to sell, and then these women could make a little extra Christmas money. We all could take a few hours in the store," she mused, "like a cooperative."

"I love you, Abbey, and I especially love this new woman you've become," Sam said, putting his hand on her waist again. "I will support any idea that you have. Now let's get something to nibble on so we can get back to what we did earlier before my wife shows up!"

She fixed him a quick ham sandwich with some macaroni salad. When he was finished, he rose to put his plate in the sink and Abbey turned, smacked him on his rear, and then darted up the stairs with her husband in hot pursuit.

❖

Chapter Fourteen

Present Day

Melissa sat on a milk crate at the back door of the restaurant, letting the cool night air dry her sweat. It had been a very busy Friday night. She felt good and satisfied that all the food went out looking great and tasting great. She was happy with her new relationship with Tristan and smiled with the thought of him. The executive chef and she were old working friends and knew how to complement each other's work. In the last few months of working here, she had gained several hours each week. She was now putting in nearly sixty as the restaurant gained in popularity. She hadn't much time for Tristan these days, since he usually left before she got up. They had a few hours here and there to make out and hold each other, and a few rainy days when his jobs were shut down for the day. This career has always been so draining on relationships in the past, she thought, no wonder I'm still a single girl!

A waitress came to the back door. Mel turned and said, "Do you have an order?"

"No, the owner would like to see you, honey. He's at table 54." She turned and left.

Hot blood coursed through her veins as she immediately thought the worst. I hope he doesn't have a complaint.

Lissa took off her soiled apron and re-applied her lipstick. She washed her hands and pulled off her hairnet. She approached Jim Burke's table and introduced herself.

"So glad to finally meet you, Melissa," he said, putting his hand out to shake hers. "Have a seat with us. This is my lovely wife, Christy."

"So happy to meet you; I love your dress, Christy," Lissa said with sincerity.

"Thank you, Melissa. Excuse me, darling, I am going to powder my nose while you talk business," said the bored Mrs. Burke.

"Melissa," Jim said with a very serious inflection, "as you know, I have four restaurants, and I am looking to open a fifth one soon. I've noticed your influence on the dishes since the minute you arrived. You're creative and think out of the box when it comes to presentation and flavor."

Lissa cleared her throat and said clearly, "Thank you."

"Well, like I said, I'm looking for a partner on my fifth restaurant, and if you are interested, I would like you to be the executive chef in the project. I take very good care of my chefs because I know the business. I grew up in a family restaurant, and chefs usually moved from season to season." He paused. "So I try to make it worthwhile that they stay."

"Yes, chefs are like fine artists, always searching for the bigger and better," Melissa added with a large friendly smile. She was excitedly gripping her leg with one hand under the table. "Actually, sir, I am also looking for a partner, and I have a plan started. Just ideas on paper, not an actual business plan."

"Well, that sounds great. Do you have the capital to back this? I know you have the talent."

"Yes, I have some."

Christy came back to the table and asked if he or Lissa would like some wine. They both declined.

"Okay, Melissa. Can you meet with me Monday morning at my office and we can go over the ideas that you have?"

"Yes. Is nine in the morning too early for you?"

"No, that's fine. I need to get back here for deliveries."

❖

Chapter Fifteen

Present Day

Melissa left the table with a refreshing sense of excitement in her mind. She wanted to tell everyone and no one. She did want to sit down with the two people in the world who mattered to her, Tristan and Karen, and tell them.

She was scheduled off on Sunday that week, so it gave her some time to format a better business proposal. A big storm was brewing down in Florida and was expected to reach New Jersey by the weekend, so the restaurant would be slow enough to be off. Lately even when she was scheduled off, she still came in to check on the dessert girl and the salad girl.

❖

Chapter Sixteen

Present Day

K aren and Lissa spent the early morning shopping flea markets. They lugged some of the treasures that Karen had bought into the house. One item was an old oak deacon's bench that she wanted to strip and redo. Karen had said to put it in the hallway until Tristan got home and they could take it downstairs.

The rain had started at noon just as forecasted. It came down heavily with strong winds, only lessening briefly. It was another Nor'easter.

The next morning, Melissa, Karen, and Tristan met in the kitchen for coffee, eggs, and pancakes. Tristan gave Mel the day off from cooking. Karen would be rushing out to teach student bible studies before church. Lisa and Tristan had no plans. Lissa was just looking for a nap somewhere in the day.

They sat, enjoying breakfast, and Karen told Tristan of the treasures that she had acquired. Mel reminded Tristan to help her carry the deacon's bench into the basement for Karen's winter project. They discussed the restaurant offer that Mel had and they gave their advice. Basically, they advised her to go with the man as a partner and investor, but to make sure she had a good lawyer in real estate and business contracts before she started. They also told her they thought it was a win-win situation since he had built successful businesses before and had financial backing. They enjoyed each other's company in Karen's sunny kitchen as the dark gloomy rain came down.

❖

Chapter Seventeen

Present Day

Tristan and Lissa cleaned up the breakfast dishes. They kissed and touched each other as they accomplished the chore. It had been a few weeks since Lissa had spent any real time with Tristan.

They brought their laptops down to the oak kitchen table to work. Melissa wanted to polish up her presentation for her meeting with Jim Burke. After an hour had gone by, Tristan got up and asked Mel if she would like a cup of iced tea. He came over and kissed her on the back of the neck and then licked her ear. This sent a shiver down to her toes and woke up her spirit. She turned and started kissing him as she slowly rose up to her feet. She slid her arms around him and he did the same to her. The immediate passion was carried to her bedroom.

They laid there afterward holding each other. Melissa said, "This is another fine mess you've gotten me into, Lucy!" and they both giggled.

A few more minutes went by, and Tristan said, "Karen will be home from church soon. We should get up and get dressed. And we need to take that bench into the basement for her."

"Yeah, she'll wonder what we've been doing all afternoon while she was teaching."

They got dressed and made the bed. They met down in the hall near the basement door as Karen came through the back door. "Need help?"

"Yeah, can you get the door and light; we'll lift," Tristan said.

"How was church today?" asked Mel.

"It was good. I only had five kids show up for bible school, but we had twenty-five people show up for service." Karen followed them into the basement with the bench.

"Where do you want it? Would over on that wall under the light be good?"

"Hey, look at the water!" cried Mel.

"I thought this basement was always dry," said Tristan.

The three of them went over to the wall to investigate where the small stream was coming from.

"Look at this bookcase; it isn't sitting on the floor, but hanging off a metal rail. Let me see if I can push it over." He put his weight into the shelf, but it didn't budge in either direction.

"Maybe we should take off these few canning jars first," chimed Karen.

"It's nailed shut. I wonder what's behind it." She turned and looked at Tristan, and at the same time they both said, "sawzall!" and they giggled as they both headed up the stairs to Tristan's truck.

Karen was left standing in the basement saying aloud to no one, "What's a saw all? Well, I guess I could get a flashlight. Maybe change into jeans and a tee shirt."

Within minutes, the trio was back to work. Melissa carried the extension cord and Tristan carried a long plastic box. Mel started taking the bottles and jars off of the shelves.

"So that's a saw all?"

"Actually, a sawzall or reciprocating saw. We'll have the nails cut behind the shelves in no time," Lissa said proudly, looking fondly at Tristan, who had told her about the tool.

The sawing only took a few minutes as the single blade hacked its way through the nails. Tristan put the saw down in the plastic box and took the flashlight from Karen, who had changed into jeans and a tee.

"When did you get changed?" Tristan asked, expecting no answer in reply. This time when he put his weight on the shelf, it moved to the right. A squeal of wheels not oiled in many years groaned but gave way.

❖

Chapter Eighteen

Present Day

Light beams picked up many cobwebs at first, and then large objects in this secret room. The three stood unmoving, thoughts of a buried treasure going through their minds. The smell of moist, musty decay of years gone by attacked their senses with a vengeance. Karen started sneezing.

"I've read stories of people in the 1930s burying money in their basements, but this is different," Mel offered to dead silence. She placed her hand over her nose to protect it from the overwhelming musty odor.

"We need more light. I see wiring running in that room, but it's the old knob-and-tube kind. I wouldn't chance it. I'll get my big hundred-thousand-watt light out of my truck."

"I'll get a broom for the cobwebs. What's a knob and tube?" Karen said.

"I'll get the shop vacuum from the attic," Melissa said, "and my camera. This is some cool shit."

A few minutes passed, and once again the adventurers were back. Karen had on a ski hat, latex gloves, a rain coat, and goggles for the spiderwebs. Melissa laughed at her friend's look and patted her back for her bravery.

"You go, girl!" she said as she shot a few digital pictures of the space and one of her friend's costume.

"What is that thing in the middle, Tristan?" Karen asked with scared concern. "Is it asbestos or something? Is it an old heater?"

Tristan ran the flashlight along the pipes, which ran into barrels. He started laughing.

Mel, who was investigating a few boxes in another corner with a flashlight, said "Hey, look, formulas!"

"Why are you laughing, Tristan?" Karen asked with a degree of annoyance and fear.

"It's your plain, old-fashioned, everyday still."

"Still what?" Karen asked.

"You know, Karen, for making whiskey, a still," Mel said. "I wonder if there's any aged booze in it."

"By its green patina, I'd say it's made from copper. It looks like they used to drip the whiskey into these oak barrels. See how they're up off the floor with a spigot on them for draining? They're green with mildew now, but they were probably beautiful oak. The same with that green copper still over there; we could clean that up. I wonder if it's worth more as scrap or as the antique still that it is." Tristan stopped. He realized that he was rambling on and might be frightening Karen, and where was Mel? "Melissa, where are you?"

"I'm over here, behind the barrels. I found some old formulas for Philadelphia bourbon whiskey and different liquors, like gin," she mumbled, holding a flashlight with her chin and shoulder. She was sitting on an old crate.

Karen was still busy sweeping away cobwebs. She was trying to not be stressed out by this new discovery of leaks, asbestos, and lord knew what else. The other two seemed so excited about the find. Karen said, "Did you find anything else in here?"

Tristan said no, that it was a pretty clean room except for a few wooden boxes of bottles, a stopper machine, a box of paperwork, the wooden barrels, and the still itself. The room was a good size, and he was trying to figure out the construction of it—the purpose of it and the location of it to the house. He said that he found out why the water was coming in. There was an old vent that must have taken in water, and he would trace it in the morning for Karen and get it sealed up.

Melissa, being the chef, wanted to examine the recipes more closely. She wanted to take the box up to the kitchen. She loved history and wanted to preserve this find as much as possible. She also had in the back of her mind the meeting in the morning with Mr. Burke. The three friends spent an hour down in the secret room, and then decided to wash up and order cheese steak hoagies for dinner.

Melissa spent the rest of the night at the table with Tristan, pondering the formulas book and how life was back in the 1920s. The big find had superseded her preparing for the big Burke meeting.

❖

Chapter Nineteen

Present Day

Melissa met Mr. Burke at his office, which could have passed as a real estate office in a strip mall. It was tastefully decorated in a colonial theme and not overly pretentious. He offered her coffee and sat down to listen to her spiel about her restaurant idea. She explained to him the barbecue concept. She wanted to create the illusion for the customer of being out of town or down south without him actually leaving town. She said that while working across the country, she had gained quite a few great recipes and that her last position at the Moody Gardens Hotel in Galveston prepared her for this next adventure.

Mr. Burke was polite and listened carefully. He asked what kind of money she had to offer. He told her that he had a different concept in mind but would consider hers. His was a fresh twist on food incorporating Asian qualities into blue-collar food. He said he felt this was the newest trend coming this way in the restaurant world. She politely listened to his ideas. She also promised to keep the meeting confidential.

When Melissa left the meeting an hour later, she had mixed emotions. Although he had been polite and businesslike, she felt that he wouldn't look twice at her idea. He had listened intently but had pooh-poohed her ideas aside. He didn't seem open to her thoughts. She also felt that he was in it for the money but did not have his heart in it. If it wasn't good for him financially, then he wasn't interested. So her balloon of excitement about the meeting had a small leak in it. I won't become another slave to another rich owner, she thought, slamming her fist down on the steering wheel of the Explorer.

She decided to do this project on her own, shaking her head in a gesture of assurance. Maybe her brothers could front some funds, and a small bank loan with her savings could help. If she started slowly, she could accomplish it. She knew she could. "Damn!" she yelled from inside the car. "I can do it!" Suddenly she knew and felt better about her decision.

She decided to stop at the Shop Rite and buy the components for a really nice dinner for her two best friends to celebrate the decision.

❖

Chapter Twenty

1922

The morning was a mixture of mist and continuous light rain. The warm days and cold nights created a light fog in some areas. Dick Shutter was on his way down to Philadelphia for his usual Monday meeting with his regional field supervisor, Captain Jack. He had nothing to report. He knew that there was some distilling going on in the area, but how could he get into the houses to find the source? Maybe he should go back to his clerk job in West Virginia; at least he knew what he was doing there. He knew he wasn't trusted by the locals by the way they acted hush-hush around him. He was a bit intimidated by the whole idea of being alone out here. He missed his few friends and the good food of West Virginia. What the hell was he doing up here eating cornbread for breakfast?

The office was so short on G-Men that they kept the teams in the cities and sent individuals out to the small towns. He wasn't sure he could defend himself against an irate farmer who had bigger guns than he did. He didn't want to lose his job, either. This job had given him a sense of empowerment.

Just as he rounded the curve, a deer jumped out in front of his

Packard. He tried to swerve, but the deer launched at him. The damage was done and the deer was dead. He stopped for a minute to get control. His hands were shaking. Had he screamed like a girl? What kind of G-Man was he? His front light was smashed to bits, and there was deer blood all over the hood of the car. Tufts of fur were imbedded in the trim of his broken light. He dragged the deer by the feet to a drainage ditch. Great, he thought, now I'll have to get the light fixed. A little shook-up, Dick got back in his car for the meeting in town.

The meeting with his field supervisor didn't go well. Captain Jack Blanchard had been a New York City detective before joining this new government agency. He now headed up the Philadelphia office. He acted as if Dick hadn't done anything.

"What was I supposed to do, go into their houses?" argued Dick.

"Yes!" bellowed Captain Jack, pounding his fist into the desk. "Observe their activities, sit and watch, watch, watch. They will slip up, and that's when you can jump in and arrest them. Do you still have your gun and handcuffs? The next time I see you, I want progress and not just a report that you had a hunch. Your job is on the line here, Dick. Do whatever it takes. I want a better, more aggressive report from you next Monday, or else!"

What a lousy day this was turning out to be, Dick thought. How should I complete my job? Why can't they send someone to help me? The rain came down heavier on his trip back north from Philly. His wipers barely pushed the water away from the window. And the roof leaked in his old car.

Maybe he could become friends with them. Maybe he should just do what he had been doing, and that was really nothing, until he got fired or until they moved him to a desk job. He wiped the corners of his mouth and continued watching the road for more surprise deer. Knowing how his luck was going today, he thought that maybe another one would have his sights on him.

❖

Chapter Twenty-One

1922

The day was crystal clear after the long, dreary Monday. Abbey was happy for the sunshine. She hummed her favorite tune as she packed up her candles, supplies for cleaning, and fabric for displaying items. She noticed a car across from the house. That little man from town was sitting in it. Why was he out there? Abbey felt a chill run up her back. It was the G-Man! She went up to the third floor where the housekeeper, Mary, was dusting and showed her the car across the way. The housekeeper thought that she should call Sam.

"I don't know, ma'am; I haven't seen him around before."

"No, we haven't done anything. I don't want to worry Sam. Just keep an eye on him," Abbey said, not looking at her but out the window. She stood holding the lace curtain another minute, watching the little Scaramouch light another cigarette. He was now standing, leaning against his crooked car. Abbey straightened up and went back to working on her packing. I look bigger and stronger than he does, she thought.

There was a protective anger building inside her. It was an anger that could kill to defend her family. She wasn't normally like this, but this little insect needed to be squashed before it bred more.

The scents from her candles relaxed her, and she soon forgot about the little Scaramouch. She lit a lemon-cinnamon candle, her favorite. The aroma soon filled the air. She slowly packed her crates and started to load her boxes into the huge Peerless car. Mary, the housekeeper, came down to help her. Abbey grabbed her long overcoat and headed for the car. She could see the little man watching her every move.

She headed down the road towards town, the little G-Man in tow. When she got to the straightaway just before the village, he overtook her car and pulled her over. I could run his little car over, she thought.

"What are you doing?" she screamed. "Are you trying to kill me?" Rolling the window down only halfway, she cried indignantly, "How dare you pull me over like this? Do you mind telling me what you want and why you have been parked in front of my house for three hours?"

"I am going to have to search your crates, Mrs. Rhoades," said the G-Man, brandishing an official-looking badge.

"What kind of officer are you?" she asked through the half-cracked window, pretending not to know what this guy actually did.

"I work for a section of the government, in revenue. May I look in your boxes and search your car?"

"No," came a defiant response.

"I have every right to. Do I need to handcuff you and let the rest of the villagers see this?"

"Okay, okay!" she said. "But be quick about it!"

"Please stand over by my car while I go through your crates."

She watched the fast-moving river to the left as he went through her things in the back seat of the car. She crisscrossed her coat tightly closed and crossed her arms over her chest in a secure puritan gesture. What did he have on Sam and her? They would have to be careful in case there were other G-Men out there, but she wasn't afraid of this little bug, even though he was scaring her now.

He was really surprised to find candles, jars filled with wax, fabric, rags, and soap. He had expected to find boxes of bourbon. He was almost certain that the Rhoades family was the link to the Philadelphia bourbon source. Captain had a snitch who had told him what town it was coming from. He turned to Abbey, who was still holding her coat around her waist tightly.

"My apologies, Mrs. Rhoades; I am sorry for the inconvenience. You may be on your way."

"I will be telling Sam about this the minute I get to the restaurant. He may kick you out of your room!" she threatened.

❖

Chapter Twenty-Two

1922

___

When she pulled up next to the restaurant, Abbey could see that Sam was incredibly busy. People had been shut in by the rain all the day before and now were out and about in the bright sunshine enjoying a barbecue lunch. The G-Man had followed her to the restaurant and parked across the street, still observing her. Damn little bug, she thought. She went to check and see if she could clear tables and pour sweet tea.

When she came out of the restaurant two hours later, the little bug was gone, and she had forgotten him in the lunch rush. She went and opened up her little store and started unloading her crates of cleaning supplies. She was humming to herself again. Later on, she opened the back door to take out a bin of burnable trash. The Scaramouch bug was in the alley waiting for her or Sam, she wasn't sure whom.

"What are you doing back here?" she asked defiantly.

"I'm just doing my job and observing," he replied, wiping the corners of his mouth with his fingers.

She dumped the items into Sam's burning pit and went in through the restaurant back door. She was able to get Sam aside from taking his inventory to tell her whole day to him. He listened to every word without interrupting her. She loved that about him. He also always had time for her, and that made her feel important.

"I think we need to slow down making the juice for a while," she said.

"The juice. And where did you hear that expression?" he said with a smile, putting his clipboard down. He placed his hands on her waist and pulled her close to him.

"Sam," she cried, "I'm scared, and I'm very serious."

"Well, you are right, but you look so delicious I had to touch. Go back next door and I'll be over soon. We can follow each other home."

"But you have Rotary Club tonight, and Mary is feeding the children; I thought I might stay and wipe down the shelving with bleach and get it ready for painting."

"Then how about you waiting for me to finish dinner with the guys and I'll follow you home from there. Can I make you a chicken sandwich?"

"I would love that! I haven't eaten all day, and once I start my project I'll never stop to eat." Abby sat down on a stool in the small commercial kitchen and began to tell Sam about her little bug day and discussed what they should do.

They decided to ignore the bug for now. They would still keep brewing, but they would be more careful about transporting the pork boxes. Abby felt better with some food and a chance to talk to Sam. She was ready to get to work in her store now, and he had to get over to the Rotary meeting at the tavern.

She felt like a million dollars walking into her very filthy, dusty shop next to Sam's place. It was hers, all hers. She had an attorney draw up the appropriate business papers in her name. She got goosebumps up her arm just thinking about it. She actually owned something that was hers alone.

She took a hanky out of her pocket and tied back her short curls. She got to work wiping down the shelving, walls, ceilings, and floor. She had hired a twenty-year-old neighbor kid to come help her start painting in the morning. Soon she would be open for business, she thought with a huge smile on her face. Oh, how she loved Sam for escorting her in this direction.

She looked up from the floor that she had been scrubbing to find a figure watching her. She stopped for a second. She hadn't realized that it was now beyond dusk outside. She shivered, remembering her encounter with the G-Man earlier that day and then just as quickly shrugged it off. She thought, I'm bigger than that little bug, and I can squash him. She rose to her feet ready to fight and turned to see Sam leaning against the doorway watching her work.

"My beautiful wife, are you ready to go?"

❖

Chapter Twenty-Three

Abbey, 1903

A bigail was just a young girl of fourteen in charge of watching her younger brother after school. They lived in a small one-bedroom apartment in a row home in Brooklyn. Every day after school, Abigail would wait for her little brother at the grade school and walk him home. They would sit and do lessons together, and then he would go down and sit on the stoop while she started dinner for Mother.

Her mother worked in the women's department at R.H. Macy & Company. She felt lucky to have a job in the new fancy dry goods store. Six days a week, her mother would take the bus to 34th Street and Herald Square. Occasionally, she would take Abigail and her brother John into the city with her to visit where she worked. John loved riding all four escalators as far up as he could go, and then he would ride the elevators. It was the tallest building they had ever been in—nine whole stories.

Today, Abigail was fixing pasta and a pear and gelatin salad for Mother, who would arrive home at 6:30. The brass spigot in the tiny kitchenette came off. She went down to the building manager, Mr. Kopachewski, and knocked on the door, as her mother had instructed her to do if she had a problem. Timidly, she knocked. He answered the door with a bottle of beer in his hand. His trousers were unzipped and his suspenders rested over a thin holey undershirt. She could see his hairy belly poking through the hole.

Abigail explained that the spigot fell off and that the water was running—could he shut it off? He finished his bottle of beer. He closed the door and when it reopened, he had a dirty wooden box in one hand and a new bottle of beer in the other. Together they climbed the steps to the second-floor apartment. Abigail led Mr. Kopachewski over to the sink and stood off to the side. He placed his grubby toolbox on the table and pulled out a small screwdriver and a brass screw. In minutes, the spigot was fixed. He had done this all without saying a word to Abbey.

He turned to her and suddenly began conversing. He said she was very beautiful and what a grown-up girl she was. He kept inching closer to her as he talked. "My, my, you're so pretty." He moved his hand up and touched her hair, slightly brushing her cheek. Why didn't she ever come down and visit him? Where was her brother? Boy, what a beautiful young lady she was. Did she have a beau in her life?

He was just inches from her. She felt cornered by the counter and the wall. He stunk like beer and bad body odor. He started to press his large torso to her dress. She slowly reached her hand to the counter. His right hand was lifting the hem of her dress. She could hear herself say "please stop," but she wasn't sure she was saying it aloud. She knew she was saying it over and over, louder and louder, but she was still so scared that she didn't know if it was being heard. His hand was now in her panties. Her hand found a small steak knife that she was using to trim the pears. This gave her the encouragement and power to speak aloud.

He had her skirt all the way up now, and she could feel something hard against her body. She said loudly to Mr. Kopachewskli, "Stop or I'll stab you!" He ignored her voice, and she repeated it as he pressed even closer to her: "Stop or I'll stab you!" She took the knife and with one large swing stabbed the smelly old manager in the arm. He screamed like a girl and stepped back. He stared at her as if he would hit her.

She was still holding the bloody knife tightly. "I'll use it again!" she said loudly. He turned, holding his arm and forgetting his toolbox. He yelled a few words in Polish and English that she had never heard before, but she understood the word "bitch." He left.

When she calmed down and washed up, she quietly took his toolbox and beer and put it in front of his door. She went out and got her brother, who was playing marbles in the alley with a friend. Her mom would be home in half an hour. He was to get washed up, she instructed as he protested. She just didn't want to be alone. She guessed she should tell her mom what had happened. Would they have to move? Mom had such a great job, and the rent there was cheap.

Her mom listened to the story, and she left nothing out. Mom said that she would call the owner of the building in the morning on the way to work and let him decide what to do about Mr. Kopachewski. A few days later, Mr. Kopachewski was moving out when she got home from school. She kept her head up and held her brother's hand tightly. She noticed that he was still wearing an undershirt with a hole in it, but now his arm was bandaged. She had a small smile on her face as she quickly made her way up the stairs.

She thought to herself, You were right, mister, I *am* all grown-up now.

From that day on, she would never let another man come near her until the summer she met Sam, who was visiting with his aunt across the street. He was a nice shy boy from Pennsylvania. They talked all that summer and wrote all that winter to each other. The following summer, they started courting, and that winter he asked for her hand in marriage. The following spring after high school was finished, they were married.

Chapter Twenty-Four

Present Day

Melissa arrived home to Karen's house at three o'clock, her arms filled with groceries. She had chicken breasts and champagne, ham, cheese, and fennel. This was going to make a really nice dinner. Everyone should be home tonight. She called Tristan and told him briefly about the meeting and said that she would be making a special dinner. He jokingly said that he would be home on time and hungry, but not for her cooking. Karen said she could leave a half an hour early today because she had skipped lunch, so she was already starving.

Lissa made chicken breasts smothered in a champagne sauce, covered in capicola ham and Jarlsberg cheese, baked fennel, and fresh broccoli with roasted red peppers. It was a beautiful dish. The appetizer for her hungry friends was Gouda cheese, fresh apples, and grapes with a honey sour cream sauce.

Tristan brought home a bottle of Pleasant Valley Foundry Red made in the Finger Lakes, which was a perfect accompaniment to the dinner. Karen even had a half-glass. Tristan sat next to Lissa and often found her leg under the table, squeezing it occasionally. The three sat at the table until late, discussing her ideas and all of the possibilities. She felt that her dream was becoming more of a possibility. Karen offered a small loan of $5,000 that she had set aside in a vacation fund, but said as long as she was alone, she didn't want to vacation. Tristan offered to become her partner in the restaurant, which meant free contracting for her. He also said that if this last job came in on time, with his savings he could put up $10,000. Melissa said if she cashed in her CDs she could put up $7,000. The restaurant was taking shape.

Karen said she would help put a business plan together and suggested an organization run by women in business to look at her plan before approaching a bank. It should go pretty quickly with the Internet, Karen pointed out, to look up prices of items such as glassware and smokers and such. Lissa was so excited she couldn't wait to start. Tristan got up and started clearing the dishes and offered ice cream to the girls. He said it was one thing that he could make.

Karen headed upstairs, leaving her two friends to wash up and have some privacy. She had noticed Tristan touching Lissa whenever he could.

The next morning, Lissa called the realtor to make an appointment to see the building in town. She just felt drawn to it. She met Tristan in the afternoon at the building, and the realtor let them in. She had asked what they intended to do in the building, and Lissa answered "A restaurant," but did not go into details. The realtor said that it used to be a restaurant years ago but it had been closed for most of this decade and that it was time to bring it back. She also said that the insurance office next door would soon become available if they wanted to knock down a wall for more dining area.

Things were definitely progressing smoothly. Lissa always believed that if things fell into place without much difficulty, then she was doing the right thing. She also had a feeling of déjà vu when she walked into the back area that used to house the kitchen. She had an overwhelming sensation of having been here before. Yes, this was meant to be, she told herself. Tristan came up behind her and held her hand tightly in support.

"I like it, Melissa," he whispered. Then he turned to the realtor and said, "May we see the basement? I need to check the construction."

Two weeks went by and the business plan was put together. Karen was polishing the final touches. Tristan had offered his floor plan, lumber, plumbing, and electrical list. Lissa was hoping that the bank would lend them more than what they were backing so they wouldn't have to bother her brothers for loans. It was a good time of year.

Tristan had to go into the basement and looked in on the still just sitting there, quietly forgotten again in the excitement of the restaurant venture. He yelled up for Lissa. She came running down, worried that Tristan had fallen or something. She found him standing there at the entrance to the secret room, bobbing his head. She came up and stood next to him.

"What's wrong; did you see a mouse?" she said with a smirk, poking him in the side.

He grabbed her by the waist and pulled her towards him. He said, "Look," as he steered her in the right direction.

"There's the gimmick you're always talking about, right here in front of us. We could polish it up. The whole theme of the restaurant could be done in the 1920s. The bartenders could dress like gangsters and the waitresses like flappers. We could do a speakeasy type bar menu, serve mason jars of hooch, and polish up the still and use it as the centerpiece in the dining room."

He was rambling on so fast that it took her by surprise, but she got the drift of what he was saying. It was exactly the catch or gimmick that they needed. The formulas could even go on display, she thought, thinking back to that book she had found. In the back of her mind, she was hoping that Karen would let them use it, since technically it was hers.

Chapter Twenty-Five

Abbey and G-Man, 1922

A bbey was packing bottles in butcher paper and crating them up. Sam was taking them up and out of the back door of the house. He would cautiously look around for the Scaramouch.

What the G-Man would never know is that when he had come to town and rented a room from Sam, Sam had bought Abbey a newer used car. He had taken out the back seat and built in a secret box under it, using the same fabric. When he put the seat back in, a portion of this secret box went into the trunk of the car. It blended so well that the average person would never know this addition under the seat had been made. The optical illusion would only be discernible to the designer of the car.

The time that Dick Shutter, the G-Man, had stopped Abbey, he only looked through the boxes that were on the top of the seat and didn't lift the seat cushion up. There, he would have found six crates holding 144 bottles of sweet golden Philadelphia bourbon. They were all nicely wrapped in brown butcher paper resembling loins of pork.

Now, the hard part about the transportation of liquor was unloading the pork boxes. Usually, Sam would just put them in his smoke house and no one was the wiser when the butcher came to load the crates back in his truck. Now with the G-Man in the back apartment, he had a view of the entire back of the building, so Sam and Abbey had begun meeting Jake in different locations. Once they met up at the bee farmer's house since he lived on a quiet back road. They met another time at an old Civil War park and another time closer to the city at an underpass. Once the butcher had come up to the house, but Abbey was nervous about this and had a bad feeling, so they didn't do the transport this way again. Sam didn't understand her logic since they were loading the cases themselves almost daily, but he learned over the years not to argue with a woman's inner feelings because it was a lost cause.

A few times, Sam had watched Dick Shutter drive off, usually on Monday mornings. This was a day when they moved as much as they could, especially ingredients. They still watched carefully in case other G-Men were sent out: After all, Dick Shutter wasn't their best. Sam had to devise a plan to get the man out of the back apartment. He thought about shutting off the toilet or the water and moving him to the front apartment and wondered if he would be suspicious of these actions.

❖
Chapter Twenty-Six

Sally, 1922

S ally had known Sam for most of his life. She didn't remember
when they had met; she just knew he was a good, fair soul. She had
been working for him for about six months now. When Sally's
husband had passed suddenly, Sam came to her and said if there was
ever anything he could do, to let him know. He said it with such warmth
and sincerity that she knew he meant it. So after several months of grief,
cleaning up, and putting things in order that her husband had left
unattended, she was happy to get out of the house. The farm was paid
for, luckily, as it had been in her family before Stan.

It was a long road to independence for her after his death. She was
rebuilding her life. She awoke one day and started packing up any
remains from her life with Stan. It wasn't always a good life and now she
had a fresh start. She was happy.

Over the past few months, she had been watching Sam do some crazy
things. A few early mornings she had watched him unloading pork boxes
from his car to the smoke house. Then in the late evenings or when it was
quiet in the afternoons, he would load up his car with cracked corn, sugar,
and honey from the restaurant. Sometimes he would only take one bag

at a time into the car, and then wait an hour or two to take another. She pondered his movements for a while until she figured it out. She watched him and protected him for the friend and boss that he was. After all, he had saved her life, in a way, by putting her to work.

So when that little fly, Dick Shutter, walked into Sam's restaurant last month, she had become concerned for Sam's wellbeing. Up until now, she hadn't told Sam that she knew he was making hooch. They had never even discussed whether she had a wet or dry house. In actuality, she had quite the wine and gin cellar left by her late husband and polished off a few every day.

Sally went out to the back of the restaurant to see Sam. There weren't any customers in the dining room at the moment. She knew there was a dilemma going on. Abbey and he were having lots of discussions as of late. It was time to offer Sam some help. Sam was moving something around in the back of the car, in the alleyway, for Abbey.

"Sam," said Sally, lighting up a cigarette, "I'm just going to come right out and speak my mind." The stout, well-endowed woman pulled in a long puff of smoke and tucked a long stray grey hair back with the other hand.

"Sally, you aren't going to leave me now, are you? I thought you were happy," Sam said, turning and wringing his hands clean.

Abbey was approaching the car and said, "What's going on?"

"I care a lot about you folks. You've become family to me since my husband passed away. I know that you're brewing hooch at night, and I'm willing to help you as much as I can. You're my family now. So what's the problem?"

Abbey came over and gave Sally a big hug. "Well, we've been trying not to get caught by that snoopy bug upstairs. We used to bring the boxes of whiskey down here, and the cute butcher Jake would pick up the crates. Well, now we have to try not to do it here. That little bug watches us too often," she said in hushed tones close to Sally's ear.

"I see," said Sally, taking another puff and pondering the process. She blew out a long line of smoke and coughed, vibrating her ample bosom. "Well, seeing how my tin-can Ford is out of the barn and here each day at work, you can unload the juice in my barn, then give me a ride into work until this G-Man hits the road. I could get some work done at Nick's garage on the Lizzie. The car is rattling so much when I finally get it started that I feel like my teeth will fall out. You'd think it would shake off some of this fat. Could you get Jake to pull in and pick up from my barn?" She drew in another long breath of smoke.

"Sally, I can't believe you're offering all this to us," Sam said, pulling his hanky out of his back pocket and clearing his nose. "I think it could work, at least for a while. How about if I pick up the cost of your car repair?"

"*That* I will take you up on, Sam. Hey, did you hear that they're going to start building magnets in the bottom of the Model Ts?"

"No, I hadn't heard that, Sally; what will that do for the car?"

"It'll catch all of the parts that it loses running down the road." Sally laughed a hearty deep laugh and had to put her hand on her chest to slow down the pace of her breasts as the laugh fell into a cough. "Hey, maybe I could try a bottle of your brew sometime? I'm getting tired of wine and gin every night! Something a little warmer would be nice."

"Oh, Sally, we love you!" Abbey cried, and put her arms around her friend for a quick hug.

❖

Chapter Twenty-Seven

1922

T he next morning, Sally, Abbey, and Sam met out at the barn. It looked good and secure for the transfer. Sally's farm was located down a long, winding driveway that made it barely noticeable from the road. But at this time of year, the trees were thinning down as the winter slowly approached. It would be more noticeable before long.

It was a large red barn designed for holding farm equipment or carriages with a few horse stables on each side. Garage doors were at each end of the barn so that tractors could drive in and out without reversing. This was probably a design that was held over from the horse-and-buggy days, so you could pull the team of horses in, unhook them, and pull the wagon out the next morning without having to turn it around. Small windows lined the top rafters to add some light to the barn. Tools were hung neatly up and out of the way.

Sam stood and thought and looked as Sally and Abbey conversed about her latest candle combinations. Sally was offering her combinations of scent ideas. He figured the barn would work just fine. It would have to be locked after each drop in case they were followed. Two locks for two barn doors. Sally had never locked it before. The dusk was coming earlier, so Jake's pork truck coming down the driveway might not be noticed. He could unlock the barn and pull right in for privacy. There weren't any neighbors around to see too much, just a few chickens and a rooster in the end stall of the barn. Sally had sold the one remaining horse months ago.

They started the process the next day. Jake was very happy about the new arrangement. He was starting to get a little nervous about the G-Man hanging around the village. Jake was at the biggest risk because if they figured out the transportation, they could pull him over at any time on the road and they would surely find his stash of bourbon. This would cause grave jeopardy to his family, who depended solely on him for income. They would at least survive for a while on the liquid cash that he was able to stash each week. He was hoping to see his children off to college someday, so he was still willing to take the risk for the children's sake.

❖

Chapter Twenty-Eight

Present Day

Melissa put the box of papers in the sunny parlor at Karen's house. She clicked on the Dish TV to Sirius Radio, on the coffee house music station. She filled her mug with hazelnut coffee and went into the parlor to finish exploring the box.

She found a small Brownie camera, and under that was an old black leather-bound photo album. It was very fragile; some of the glue that used to hold it together had worn off. She set it down on the mahogany coffee table and carefully turned the pages of the past. She visited a family of pictures and a few mementos. A valentine card addressed to an Abbey from Sam, a few intricate Christmas cards, and a few sketches made by kids. These were in between pages of pictures of the family. She came across pictures of the house and even one of a Christmas in the very parlor that she was sitting in. She found a picture of a man working at the still. It wasn't very good; it was very dark.

One picture was of three people standing near a window that she recognized as being from the back of the building she had just looked at for the restaurant. The back of the picture said "Sam, Abbey, and Sally, Spring 1924." It had a tall, thin man standing very close to a thin woman, and a beefy, shorter woman was on the other side of the man. Another picture had Sam and Abbey posing with a cute strong-looking man, whose shirt sleeves were rolled all the way up, exposing his muscular arms. The picture was taken in front of a barn. The writing on the back of that picture said "Sam, Abbey, and Jake, Summer 1924."

The book contained many other pictures of family events, communion parties, graduation pictures, and family holidays. There were locks of baby hair tied by a ribbon and a rose wrapped in tissue paper with a Mass card.

Melissa was in her glory with this treasure left by a family who had once lived in this very house and who formerly used the building she was going to be purchasing. It was simply amazing and eerie at the same time. She wanted to find out more and incorporate as much as she could into her restaurant. She still had more items to investigate, but wanted to take her time.

She went straight to the Internet. Using an old envelope with Sam's name on it, she started her research. Surprisingly, it didn't take her very far—mostly family tree and ancestry search engines came up. So she decided to head down to the local library for more information. She loved the Internet, but it didn't always give you everything you needed unless you knew which highway to take.

She met Tristan, who was just coming in from a long day of interior trimming and woodwork. She showed him her find, still on the coffee table in the parlor. She explained that she was on her way out to the library; would he like to go with her?

"Sure, I love research like this; just give me five minutes to shower up," he said with a smile, "then afterwards I could buy you some dinner as well." With a quick kiss on the lips, he was gone.

The library was open until eight, and they worked until the librarian started slowly turning off lights. They found a pile of old newspapers and searched each one. They found a book designed by a local university on historic houses and their history around Upper and Lower Black Eddy. They found that Sam had owned the restaurant from 1918, probably opening it after returning from the war. He kept it open and worked it till 1936. They found that Abbey had owned a candle and craft store in the building next to the restaurant from 1922 through the fall of 1932, when the Great Depression hit the hardest and forced the closing of the store.

❖

Chapter Twenty-Nine

Present Day

Later that night Tristan held Mel. They talked about the future and their ideas for the restaurant. They had become very close in the last few weeks. Melissa still had trouble believing that this might be the relationship that would last. She had been down this road so many times. She still held back a little, and she felt that maybe Tristan sensed this whenever they talked about their future together. It wasn't that she didn't care for Tristan. It was just so hard to let go and trust someone after being burnt in relationships so many times.

She stroked his chest as he rambled on about the next step for the restaurant and ideas about what to name it.

"It should be unique, don't you think? Like the gimmick you're always talking about. But it should be catchy and easy to remember. Dontcha think, babe?"

She grinned at his enthusiasm and began stroking the back of his neck, massaging it as she answered, "Yeah, why don't we meet with Karen tomorrow and start putting ideas down on paper. I want to keep Karen involved as much as possible. It will help when we have that final bank meeting next week. I was also thinking of sending over a nice luncheon of smoked barbecue beef for the bank staff. This way the loan manager can get on-the-spot, real-time, honest feedback."

"That's brilliant, Mel. I know we will succeed!" he said and swung his powerful leg over hers, wrapping himself over her. It wasn't long before they were kissing and caressing each other.

She felt his manhood right away, and that sent a wave of pleasure over her loins. They were definitely a good fit for each other and the best of friends. Maybe, just maybe, they would make it this time around. They enjoyed pleasing each other and often spent several hours an evening doing so, usually when Karen was at choir or at one of her club meetings.

Chapter Thirty

Present Day

The next morning, Melissa told Karen about the names. Karen said she already had a list started. Melissa called the bank and arranged with the bank manager to bring lunch on Friday. She called her friend at the restaurant, and by offering to create a barbeque special for the menu she was allowed use his smoker for the day. Everything was falling into place.

She took the rest of the day and headed down to Philly. On Second Street under the Ben Franklin Bridge, she visited restaurant warehouses of new and used equipment. She introduced herself to the owners and made contacts. She then headed over to the stadium area to Jetro, a restaurant food supply house. Next she stopped at the wholesale fish market, and by two o'clock she was in the Italian Market on Ninth Street. She purchased enough beef and vegetables for the bank lunch. For the restaurant, she went to the game butcher, where she purchased ten fresh Cornish game hens that she would smoke together with her beef. On the way out of town, she stopped at the State Store and purchased a bottle of bourbon whiskey, which would be the catalyst in the bourbon barbeque sauce for the hens and the beef.

She headed back and pulled into the restaurant at the same time that Jim Burke pulled in.

"Hi, Melissa, how have you been? The chef tells me you're not covering for John anymore?"

"Oh, hey, Mr. Burke."

"Call me Jim, Melissa."

"Yeah, I miss working here, but I am bringing in some special hens that I picked up today. Chef Mark is going to let me work on a special for tomorrow's menu. Maybe you'll be able to sample it. Will you be here tomorrow?"

"Well, that sounds wonderful; we really do miss you here. I'll try, but if I can't make it, maybe you could save me a plate. How is your business venture coming along?" he asked in earnest as he helped her with some of the packages.

She was a little embarrassed when he looked at the big bottle of bourbon whiskey. "It's for the sauce for the hens. The bank is just about a week out for approval. I don't think they're very happy about my gypsy-like behavior. They like settled, established people, but they seem impressed with my résumé and business plan. They like my partner and the dollars that I have backing up part of the loan. The building is in purchase pending, so that's secured, and I got a really good price on it."

"Everything sounds like it is falling into place; I'm happy and sad for you at the same time."

"What do you mean?"

He held the door for her. "Your talent won't be working for me," he said with a smile.

Blushing at this compliment, she said, "Thank you, Mr. Burke."

"Call me Jim. Come join me for a glass of wine when you're done with the chef. I need to look over some paperwork. Just come upstairs to the office when you're done. I want to hear more of your ideas."

Lissa was totally impressed by his down-to-earth friendliness to her.

She would join him for a drink as soon as she called Tristan to let him know where she was. This was another weird thing she wasn't used to—checking in. The gypsy in her was used to just going for it without checking in with anyone.

The chef came around the corner, interrupting her thoughts about her relationship.

❖

Chapter Thirty-One

Present Day

After putting the hens in the walk-in and marinating the beef for smoking in the morning, she joked with Sous Chef John and Chef Mark before they got hit for the dinner hour. Chef Mark was excited about his dinner special. She headed upstairs to the office where Sandy, the bookkeeper, and Jim were talking. She knocked lightly on the door frame.

"Hey, Melissa, I'll meet you at the bar in just a few minutes, okay?"

"Sure."

Marjean, her favorite bartender, was working. Marjean was a teacher by day and a part-time bartender at night. She was in her upper forties and wore the most unique clothing combinations. It was a joy to see her ensemble each shift. Tonight she was wearing a hot pink tee shirt with a black lace top over it and finally a white lace vest over that. She had several beaded necklaces of varying lengths, in pinks and blacks, and pink beaded earrings complimented a huge smile. Mel guessed that it helped with tips. She was conversing with Marjean and having a glass of Ravines Cerise red wine when Jim came in and joined her.

"Let's sit over here." He motioned to a table off the bar area. "Marjean, can you get me a glass of whatever Melissa is drinking?"

"My friends call me Mel or Lissa; the bankers call me Melissa. So how is your new project moving along, Jim?" She thought she should start out holding the cards with this guy.

"We're moving along quite well and hope to be open in the next month or so. The kitchen is almost done, and the dining room is just being carpeted. Maybe you could come for one of our pre-opening dinners. You know, so we get the kinks out before the real opening."

"Thank you, I would love that. Do you need any help now?"

"Yes, actually we do. Why don't you stop by? We can always use the extra talent with so many details to get done. So how's your new partner doing? Who is he or she? A talented chef like you?"

"Oh no, he—Tristan—is a good friend and roommate of my best friend. He's in construction. My roommate, Karen, who has been my friend since high school, also put up some money."

"What bank are you going through?"

"The Bucks County National in Washington Crossing; it was the largest bank in the area, and it has a loan officer on site."

"Yes, the lovely Anne Green. I know her well. I'll put a good word in for you."

"Well, that would be greatly appreciated, Mr. Burke."

"Please call me Jim. One restaurant owner to another—if you ever need anything at all, just call. By the way, this is a great-tasting wine. I didn't know I carried it."

"Thanks, it's from Ravine's Winery in the Finger Lakes. I had it there once when I was vacationing. It has a hint of cherry finish. The winemaker and owner used to work for Dr. Konstantin Frank's Vinifera Wine Cellar. It was a well-known winery in the Finger Lakes of New York, one of those little pieces of information that I've come across traveling around.

"Do you know any used equipment guys? I was down in Philly

shopping today, but I'm sure there's a local guy. Also, do you know a good Ansel system guy for the venting?"

"Give my office a call in the afternoon and I'll have my secretary pull up the names. I better get home to my pretty wife. She'll be expecting me soon. Good luck with your project. I know you will do well, and don't be a stranger."

"Thank you, Jim. I promise I won't, and you and Christy are invited to my pre-opening dinners in a few months," she said, standing and shaking his hand.

❖

Chapter Thirty-Two

1922

The daylight was growing shorter, and Abbey was growing more impatient with the annoying bug. They started moving most of the crates on Mondays. Saving up the load at the house and moving it in bulk was more risky. The Scaramouch seemed to leave town on Mondays. Sam was in full speed at the house, and Jake kept asking for more. Sam was thinking about getting another barrel and still. This would double the amount that he was making.

Sam was now placing his revenue in a metal box under the front porch. His logic was that in case of a house fire, the porch would be the last thing to burn. Abbey and Sam had everything they needed—new appliances, a nice car—and it felt good to be putting cash away for a rainy day.

Abbey's business was doing quite well. People made special stops for her candles and other local treats. If they ate next door, they usually came in to browse. She kept putting her money back into more store merchandise and was thinking of advertising fall specials in the paper since it was now candle-burning season.

Jake was doing great with the barn. Sometimes if Sally was home, she came out and helped him move the crates. She had the doors unlocked before he was up the drive so that he could pull right in. She loved to flirt with the handsome driver. They were becoming good friends. She started making pies and cookies for his wife and kids. Jake had purchased a family-sized used car, but nothing flashy. His wife was now learning to drive in the evenings. This made it easier for the whole family to travel together. They could now go to Federal Street in Camden to see her family without having to borrow a vehicle.

The Scaramouch was still nearby, but he started hounding another couple on a farm a few miles north of Upper Black Eddy. The Scaramouch had moved to the Village Tavern, where they offered a different selection of food and better accommodations. The water actually worked there.

On his last trip into the city, he had asked his boss for help in what he explained to be an almost positive still site. It was located on a family farm just north of Upper Black Eddy. His boss said if he was sure, then he would send three agents up to help him raid the farm on Thursday. Dick said he had records of large purchases of mason jars and sugar. He said he had been watching the farmer from the road for a few weeks. They were definitely cooking and loading boxes and working all hours in the barn.

❖

Chapter Thirty-Three

1922, The Raid

On Thursday morning, three agents dressed in black with beige overcoats and felt fedora hats met Junior Agent Shutter. They drove in two vehicles to the police station to inform the local officer on duty. They then proceeded up to the Mauri farm. Officer Dick Shutter went to the door and knocked while the other men waited in flanks around the perimeter of the house with guns in hand. When Lena Mauri came to the door wearing an apron and holding a mason jar, Dick thought, We've got you now—evidence in your hand.

"Mrs. Mauri, G-Man Dick Shutter. May I come in? Where is your husband? Who else is home?"

"What is this all about? Who are you again? My husband is in the barn cleaning the stables. He always cleans the stables at four o'clock, and then he showers for dinner."

"May I come in?"

"Mike, Mike, come quick," she shouted as loud as she could over this short man's shoulder. This little scary-looking man was frightening her. She saw two men with guns running to her barn.

Dick pushed his way through the threshold. The other G-Man followed his lead, checking rooms in this single story house. He pounded floors with his boot and rapped on walls. The other two came pushing through with Mr. Mauri in handcuffs.

"Where's the still, Mr. Mauri? Where are you hiding it?"

"What still? What the hell are you talking about? What is all this about? What is that man doing back there pounding my walls?"

"We have word that your wife has been purchasing large amounts of sugar and mason jars. She ordered two fifty-pound bags of sugar last month alone from the local market. That's a lot of sugar to sprinkle on your cornflakes, Mr. Mauri," Dick Shutter said with one arm on his hip and an air of defiance.

"Lena, would you explain, please? These cuffs are hurting me," Michael Mauri said with a strained look on his face, his eyes focused directly on his wife.

"Oh my Lord!" Lena exclaimed loudly, "I've been putting up apple butter, peach jam, dandelion jelly, and pickles. I plan to sell half of what I make to the new store in the village—the one next to the restaurant. All of these storms have taken a toll on our pumpkin and squash crop. The extra money will come in handy. Didn't they tell you that I also purchased pectin for the jams? Oh, and I also purchased a box of cereal. Is that illegal, too?" Lena said, suddenly feeling defiant. These idiots with their matching overcoats! She had her hands on her ample hips, still holding the rim of the mason jar with her fingers.

"Let's get the hell out of here. Did you guys check the barn for trap doors?" said one of the G-Men. "How about the house?"

"Yes, everything was checked. She's got several china cabinets and mason jar boxes filled with preserves."

They all apologized to the Mauri family and left with a pair of warm handcuffs. The next day, the word about the raid gone wrong was all over town. Stills were being shut down, or their usage was down to a minimum until the coast was clear again. The fear of G-Men in Upper Black Eddy was felt by many.

❖

Chapter Thirty-Four

1922, After the Raid

A s word got out the next morning, people started stopping by to see Lena and Mike as early as six o'clock. Normally, they were quiet folk who worked hard and never had very many visitors. One of the folks who stopped by with a small pie was Sally. Lena was so happy to see her old farmer friend. She had supported Sally when her husband died suddenly last year.

"Come in, Sally," she said, extending a hug to her old friend.

"I brought you one of my green tomato apple pies; it's the last of the tomatoes from the garden and the first apples."

"Do you think we'll have the sheriff after us if we *brew* a pot of tea to go with it?" Lena said with a smirk, wiping her hands with a kitchen towel that hung off her apron.

"Why, did you steal the tea?" Both women laughed at the whole stupid experience.

"Sally, I was so frazzled after they left last night! I'm still trying to figure out why they targeted little old me," she exclaimed. She swiped a hand across her ample bosom, and then reached to tuck a stray hair in. She smiled broadly.

"Were you afraid that they might look into the woods?" Sally said, parking herself at the big round oak kitchen table.

"Oh, yes. Oh my Lordie, oh my Lordie. If they had been here earlier, they might have caught a whiff of brew coming from that shed down by the creek," she said, putting a pot of water on the stove. She gathered a ceramic pot and made a tea ball up.

"How about a fag to calm yourself?"

"Sure, thanks, Sally," and both women sat and enjoyed the smoke as the water boiled.

"That little G-Man Dick Shutter. Abbey and I call him the bug because he's always underfoot like a little bug to squash. He kept hounding her, following her. We were wondering what he had been up to. I guess we know now."

"Yeah, whatever village he came from is missing its idiot!" They both giggled.

"I just heard this one yesterday: What does a G-Man miss the most about a party?" Lena paused. "The invitation!" she answered herself, slapping her knee and getting up to retrieve the whistling tea pot and a couple dishes for the pie.

"He should go as far as a G-Man can go; the farther, the better!" The two laughed for the next hour, leaving Lena feeling much better.

When Sally got to work at eleven o'clock, she filled Sam in on the details of Lena and Mike's experience with the G-Men.

Sam said that the three G-Men left town that morning just after sun-up. He also said that the Scaramouch, as Sam liked to call him, had gotten his butt chewed out by the three men who were looking for an arrest. His boss in Philly was yelling at him on the phone. Lucy the operator had stopped in for a sandwich to-go and filled him in on the rest of the details. It was common knowledge that she knew everything happening in town first. There were no secrets in a small town, and locals always protected other locals.

By the afternoon, the G-Man excitement in the village had died down. Talk went back to the weather and when the next storm might come up the river. It had been calm for too many days now with no rain. They were in for a big one, most people agreed.

❖

Chapter Thirty-Five

1922

___

Captain Jack Blanchard of the Philadelphia District Office was quite a busy man. He sat at his chipped wooden desk too many hours a day, wondering how and why he had left New York City to work with these idiots. In the last year, he had hired more than three dozen men, whether they had experience or not, to find bootlegger stills and more. They seemed to only be bandaging the problem. It wasn't just racketeers making shine; it was also farmers and sweet little old ladies.

Captain Jack was now trying to back up his least-experienced men out in the fields with former police officers and men with military background. He wanted to keep his concentration of skilled justice men in the city, where the real gangsters lived and moved about. He had the Lanzetti brothers to focus on. Their names kept coming up regarding shootings in town, drug deals, gambling, and racketeering. He had to focus on their source for booze. He almost believed the rumor that the Lanzetti brothers were giving each row home on several blocks a still.

There was so much corruption going on that he sometimes needed a drink to get through the day. Glass and bottle companies had to be raided from time to time. Sugar and flour mills, breweries, juice factories, warehouses, and now row homes. It was too much; he could feel the grey hair just popping out.

He never told anyone, but he thought the whole law was ridiculous. There were so many people getting hurt by it: winemakers, beer makers, vineyards, sugar and yeast and corn growers, bottle companies, delivery men and liquor store owners, bartenders, bar owners. It wasn't a very well-thought-out law. Damn Volstead, he thought, but for an unheard-of $9.00 a day, he would do his best to uphold the law.

He needed two dozen more trained men to police this ever-growing disregard for the law. He needed a new speed boat or two with a serious crew to man it. He knew he had to start watching the Delaware River and Schuylkill River more closely for large shipments from the water. He had a brewery in South Philly that he had to watch constantly, as they were making 3.2% beer, which was legal as long as they weren't making a special batch with higher alcohol content. One of his junior G-Men had found some on the market.

"Such is life in Philly," he said out loud in his overstuffed, crowded, second-floor walk-up office. This was an expression that he had picked up from a series of travel books just read called *Such is Life in Coney Island* and *Such is Life in Nice*.

He started thinking about that little guy up in Upper Black Eddy and figured he'd give him another week or two before calling him down to fire him. Really, he wasn't going to make it as a G-Man. He just wasn't bright enough. He wasn't getting anywhere with those farmers. He'd probably get shot if he wasn't careful.

❖

Chapter Thirty-Six

Sally and Stan, 1900

Sally and Stan married in 1900—a new century, a new life together. Sally met Stan Janicki while visiting an aunt across the bridge in Frenchtown, New Jersey. He was tall and lean with a big head and dark, Polish heritage in his looks. She was instantly drawn to him. She was a medium-sized woman; never did she have a tiny waist, but she held a nice figure nonetheless. She had grown up as a hard-working farm girl. During their first married year together, they had lived in an apartment in Frenchtown overlooking the river. They both worked for Kings Road Winery. They were happy. When her father died a year later, the couple moved in with her mom at the farm across the river in Black Eddy.

The work on the farm was tough for Stan. It wasn't his life's dream to work so hard for so little. He was a lazy city boy. Sally hadn't discovered this when they were courting or even during their first year of marriage. Farming was a twenty-four-hour, seven-days-a-week job. Firewood had to be cut, fields had to be turned, crops brought in, horses fed, stables cleaned. Chickens and pigs had to be tended, slaughtered, and sold. There was always something to do.

Sally's mom died a year later, never having recovered from the loss of her husband. As the only surviving child, Sally inherited the farm. She gradually took on more and more jobs. She added a bigger chicken coop and became a large supplier of eggs to the market in town. She had two dairy cows and three horses, two of which were for pulling the farm equipment around. She started growing early peas that were easy to care for and put nitrogen in the soil for the pumpkin and squash crop that grew later in the summer. She would harvest this crop in the fall and put in timothy and rye for feed and for soil nutrition for the winter. She added some grapevines on the back hill, hoping Stan would take an interest in them. She grew mostly Delaware and Chardonnay grapes. She took grape-pruning classes at the winery where she used to work. This was a routine that was enjoyable. Only in the fall did she get super busy, when everything had to be harvested and turned. She brought in local boys to assist her with this. Bringing in the grapes and tying off vines had to be done. The fields had to be turned of squash to support the timothy and rye crops. It was also pig harvesting time. When the weather got cold, the old pigs had to go. The timing for her bringing in pumpkins and grapes often ran together. Still Stan showed little to no interest. She made good money selling grapes to Kings Road Winery—until prohibition.

On good days, Stan would just follow her around. He never made decisions about the farming. He couldn't care less about what they grew. If it was a rainy day, he wouldn't even get out of bed. He would just lie there and drink the day away. She said there were things to do in the barn on rainy days. Leather bridles had to be patched, horses brushed, animals fed, cows milked, stalls cleaned, tools sharpened, no matter what the weather.

As the years progressed, Sally became aware that she would not become a mother. Something was wrong with her, or it was Stan who wasn't working right. This didn't bother her; she enjoyed being outside raising her animals. They were like children to her. She was happy. Stan, however, felt more strangled as the years progressed. He had great dreams for himself, he said, but never made an effort to achieve any of them. His drinking increased to a nightly event. He started not eating dinner so that he could drink more. His personality changed when he drank. He was a mean drunk. Often Sally would just stay out of his way. By 1904, he started to hit her. At first it was just a slap across the face when she tried to get him to stop drinking. By 1915, with the stress of war and struggling crops, he was drinking and punching her regularly.

If people in town asked how she got a bruise or a scratch, she had several stories ready. The cow wouldn't cooperate, the horse wasn't into being shoed, the tractor ran under several low tree branches, or she fell over a chicken in the barn. She had many stories, but she never told a single person that it was her beloved Stan who hit her. That humiliation was just too great. For all appearances, they were a happy couple who just didn't socialize as couples often did.

She never knew what sent him into a rage. She knew it was the booze that fueled the fire. She often wondered if he was physically hurting inside. By that time, they did not share the same bedroom. Sally still cared about him. He was really all she had left of family to speak of.

During the winter of 1920, Sally was reaching her last straw with him. She was turning forty, and she was getting tired. He had been knocking her around for so many years now that she almost knew when to duck.

He had been feeling ill lately, so she took Stan down to Doctor Fitzgerald. He said that Stan most likely had the flu, as it was going around. He was running a slightly high fever, just over 101 degrees. When they got back to the house, he picked up the bottle again. She tried to stop him, and he pushed her into the dining room china cabinet, knocking her grandmother's china to the floor. Several pieces broke. She sat there crying. Sally never cried, and yet this night she just couldn't stop crying. She lay on the floor in the broken bits and cried more. She cried for the soldiers dying overseas; she cried for her friends who would never see husbands and sons again; she cried for the lacking crops; she cried for her mom, aunt, and grandmother. She cried for the loneliness of it all. She cried for about two hours.

When she had stopped crying, she went upstairs to his room, where the empty bottle was lying on the floor. She covered the passed-out Stan with blankets and tucked him in very lovingly. She then went to her mother's cedar chest and retrieved a nice feather pillow made from last season's chickens. She held the pillow tightly. Without thinking twice, she held it firmly over Stan's face. He tried to move his arms, but she had tucked the drunk in so well he couldn't reach for her. She figured it was easier than wringing a chicken's neck. She sat there on the edge of the bed for some time waiting for him to move. She almost expected him to wake up and start hitting her again.

Then a funny thing happened to her. She felt good. She took a long, deep sigh. A surge of peace and power flowed through her veins. She had just taken another life, as worthless as it had been, and she felt good. She would never be hit again. She could vote, buy appliances, drive, run a farm. She felt like a new and powerful woman. Then she wondered what to do with Stan. She put the pillow back in the cedar chest. She took another look at Stan and decided to wipe the spit off his face and tilted his head as if in a comfortable sleep. She went back down to the dining room and cleaned up the broken dishes. It wasn't like she would wake anyone up, she thought, plus she would probably have several people popping in tomorrow—friends and officials.

The next morning she got Lucy, the operator, on the phone. She told Lucy that Stan had passed on suddenly to fever, she thought, and that he had just been up to see Doc Fitzgerald. She tried to wake him this morning with no effect and he was cold. What should she do now? What should she do? she repeated to Lucy. She said she was so distraught, she was shaking. Lucy said she would make the necessary phone calls for her. The doc would have to come out to pronounce him dead, and then the funeral home would retrieve the body. Sally started to cry on the phone when she said this. Lucy completely understood.

Lucy called Lena before she called the officials. She thought that Sally could use a friend for support, someone to make her a cup of tea and comfort her. When Lena arrived at the house less than thirty minutes later, she found Sally in a house dress; her long grey hair wasn't pinned up yet. She was polishing silverware. Lena thought this a little odd at first but figured Sally was keeping her hands and mind busy.

"Do you want a cup of tea, dear?"

"Yes, that would be nice."

"Have the animals been fed?"

"Yes, I went out this morning, before I woke Stan; he likes to sleep in late, you know. Isn't this beautiful silverware? My grandmother carried it over from England on the ship, you know. I'm only missing one spoon."

"I'll make you some toast, too. I bet you haven't eaten," Lena said, looking at her friend and hoping that she would snap back. She was probably just still in shock.

❖

Chapter Thirty-Seven

Present Day

Melissa went to the restaurant early the next morning. Sandy, the bookkeeper, let her in. It was always great to see Sandy; she was such a nice person. Lissa went to the kitchen and started with the mesquite wood chips that she had soaked the night before. She placed them in the bottom of the smoker, and then she placed the beef to the left and the ten dressed hens to the right. It was a long propane smoker just outside the back door of the restaurant, in the employee's alley. It had a nice tight seal, which made it excellent for smoking. She figured the hens would be done in two hours and the beef in two and a half. While she was waiting, she got out the ingredients for rough coleslaw. She began to dice the vegetables—cabbage, purple cabbage, and carrots. She added her special secret dressing, which had white pepper and lots of sugar in it. She then went over to the stove and started to prepare the bourbon barbeque sauce. She opened cans of tomato sauce and poured this into the rendering bourbon. She added brown sugar and vinegar and a few spices. She let everything simmer for a while. She turned the fryer on to heat up.

She boiled some potatoes, then drained and mashed these in the mixer. She added a Pate a Choux mixture of butter, water, and flour to the potatoes. She added salt, white pepper, a sprinkle of cinnamon and cardamom. She then put the potato mix into a pastry bag and piped out a rope of potatoes. These she then chilled.

She grabbed a case of string beans and started making bundles. She tied them into little bunches with strips of blanched leeks. Lissa medium-diced some red peppers into little cubes to use as a garnish on the dish later. She took the scrap peppers and blended them in the food processor to create a red pepper coulis. It was a nice fresh sauce for under the string-bean package.

She pulled the chilled potatoes out and using paper strips, fried the mashed potato mixture. These could be reheated for service. She carefully laid the cooling potato on paper towels.

The chef came in to prepare for lunch. He was impressed with all she had done so far. She said, "Try my coleslaw. It has little pieces of Granny Smith apples in it. The more it marinates, the better it tastes." She showed him the gaufrette potatoes, and it was time to pull the hens out of the smoker. They were perfect. He could heat them right at service. He was so thankful to his old friend for helping him out like she did. She was also thankful for being able to use his kitchen. She was sure this luncheon was the clincher for getting the loan.

She cleaned up from behind the cooking line so Chef could do his thing and started packing up the slaw and sauce. She pulled the beef out of the smoker and started cutting and pulling it apart. She had plenty to go around. Confidence was in her blood. She still had to stop at the bakery and pick up the sesame seed rolls that she had ordered. After pulling the beef, she poured sauce over it. It tasted and smelled as good as it looked. She stored everything in her friend's cooler to be picked up in the morning. She checked with Sandy about getting in early again the following morning.

She headed to the fabric store and bought some red gingham print cloth. The next stop was Walmart to purchase a case of eight-ounce mason jars, a basket for the rolls, and a galvanized tin pot for flowers. This she could easily fit a crock pot in. She also needed some forks and napkins and small bowls for the slaw. It killed her to buy paper plates, so she went with a nice country set that sold for less than twenty dollars. Overkill, she thought, shoot the moon. She was going to borrow a pitcher from Karen for the sweet lemon iced tea.

Now all she needed was a name for her restaurant.

Later that night, she gathered her roommates in the kitchen to taste the bank luncheon that she had prepared all day. She gave them smoked barbeque beef with rich bourbon sauce on toasted sesame seed rolls with a nice pile of colorful coleslaw next to it. In mason jars she had the sweet lemon iced tea. She was hoping that the food would be the inspiration for the best name possible.

The legal tablet was filled by the time dinner was done. Some of the names were Uncle John's BBQ, Bootleggers Place, Speakeasy, Mel's Smoke House, Still Smokin', Abbey's Still, Smokey Mel's, Tristan Place, Thirsty Pete's, Copper Run, Rum Runners Paradise, and Gypsy BBQ. The three names that came to the top were Abbey's Still, since it was Abbey from the past who had led them to the future; Gypsy BBQ, since that was Lissa's nickname; and Smokey Mel's. As the last name made them imagine that Mel was a large bald man with a cigarette, it was soon dropped. They all giggled.

The three of them voted in favor of Still Smokin' and decided unanimously that the focal point of the restaurant should be Abbey's still, to honor the owner of the house and the still. They all agreed to put up any documents and pictures they had found in the basement for decoration. They also agreed that the food Melissa had prepared was right on the money and the restaurant should do very well.

They made a few more suggestions like using some flapper dresses for the waitresses and black vests with white shirts for the busboys and bartender. They were actually going to have a bar. To start with, the plan had only called for a wine and beer license, which was pending approval. They thought that the bar area should have more of a machine gun, rum runner look. Tristan said he knew exactly how to accomplish this.

❖

Chapter Thirty-Eight

Present Day

The next morning, Melissa arrived at the bank with her Ford Explorer packed. Luckily it had a door for the parking area located in the back. Unlike most banks, it also had a small kitchen area where she could set up her delicious display. She now had cards made with the name and address on them: Still Smokin' Restaurant, 57 Main Street, Black Eddy, PA.

She even remembered to borrow a bus pan and tray jack from the chef. Everything looked great. The bankers would be very impressed. She had ice packs under the coleslaw to keep the salad cold. She left the luncheon feeling good. She would be back at 2:30 to clean up. She might even poke in and say hi to Anne Green, her loan officer, and confirm next Wednesday's appointment.

She had three hours to kill, so she went to Tristan's job site to visit with José and the other guys. Maybe she could even help out for a while. She also thought about finding Jim Burke at his new restaurant.

The job site was under a lot of disorder. Plumbers and electricians were fighting for space in rooms that had to be finished. Tristan was distracted by a punch list a mile long and was trying to finish trim in the master bathroom so that the electrician could get in behind him to finish the lights and switches. The plumber was in the kitchen but soon would be starting three bathrooms, putting fixtures and toilets in. It seemed that he was answering questions every few minutes.

Melissa came in and gave her sweetheart José a kiss and Tristan a hug and kiss and told him she would catch him later. She went back to her truck and rang Jim Burke's cell number. He answered on the second ring.

"Hello."

"Hi, Jim; it's Melissa. I have a few hours of time. Could you use some help?"

"Well, sure, come on over! We just received some equipment to put away, and the shelving needs to go in place for the food delivery on Monday. We have a million things to do here."

"I'll be there in ten minutes."

❖

Chapter Thirty-Nine

Present Day

Lissa drove over the bridge to Frenchtown, New Jersey, to Jim's Restaurant on Front Street, overlooking the Delaware River. The site was majestic. It was an old mill that had been converted. He had opened the wall on the river side with large casement windows. He showed her around. He said the following spring he planned to build decks along the outside for more outdoor dining. He showed her the doorways that were already built in place for the deck entrances. People and contractors were busy with lighting fixtures, and helpers were cleaning and placing tables.

"This looks great! So where's the kitchen?"

"Right in here," Jim said, slipping behind a short wall.

She followed and was suddenly in the kitchen. The waiters had the first area inside the doors, which made sense to her, so that they could grab condiments, flatware, coffee, set-ups, and bread. The noisier part of the kitchen was around the corner, where a huge shining line could accommodate three chefs and an expediter. She could immediately see where he needed help. The kitchen was covered in fine construction dust, with boxes set all over the place.

"Mark," Jim called over to the guy checking in boxes, "this is a friend of mine. Her name is Melissa; you can call her Mel. She's a chef, too."

"Hi. Nice to meet you, Mel," Mark said, wiping his hand on his jeans and extending it to her.

"I have a few hours today and thought I'd come see if you needed some help."

"Sure, just dig in."

"Mel, I'll catch you later," Jim said, edging his way to the door.

"Okay, Jim. If I don't see you when I leave, I'll come back tomorrow to help."

"Thank you, Melissa. Every little bit helps."

Lissa spent the next few hours wiping down shelves in the store room so that inventory could be put away properly. The Department of Health was due in for an inspection sometime next week, so everything had to be just right. She was even able to mop the floor before she had to run back across the Frenchtown Bridge.

When she got to the bank, the first thing she did was stop in and see Anne Green. A secretary notified Ms. Green that Melissa was on her way back to Anne's office.

"Hi, Ms, Green. How are you doing today? Were you able to grab some of the luncheon that I brought in this morning?" Mel was holding one hand behind her back with her fingers crossed.

"Yes, and it was delicious! You really didn't have to do that. It doesn't affect your loan. I just process it and off it goes to the main headquarters," she said, trying to make it sound like she wasn't that responsible for the decision.

"But you can put a good word in for me, right? I'm a woman-owned business with many years of experience."

"Oh yes, I put your résumé in with that wonderful business plan, which was actually done quite well. I also got a phone call today from a Jim Burke. He praised your work as well. I called up to headquarters and told them that Jim Burke supported and highly recommended you. I wish I could tell you more at this time." Moving to check her calendar, she said, "Let's see." She paused. "We're scheduled for Wednesday of next week at two o'clock."

"Well, then, that sounds fine. Sorry for my excitement. I better go clean up the luncheon."

Lissa spent about half an hour gathering all her stuff. There was no food left, no signs left, not even an ounce of lemon tea. She suspected that they liked every bit of it. She would have to send over coupons and invites for the pre-opening dinners.

❖

Chapter Forty

Present Day

The next morning, Mel was up and made breakfast for Karen and Tristan. She had something to keep herself busy with today. It made her feel better knowing that things just might work out. Tristan asked if she had time to come and have lunch with him. She said that once she got to the Glass Chopstick, she would be there all day.

"That's a great name for a restaurant," Tristan said. "It is Asian-American, right?"

"Yes, I won't be home till late. Can we meet for dinner?" she said, giving him a long hug and many kisses.

"Sure." The hurt of becoming a second in her life was on his face, she thought. He, on the other hand, hoped she couldn't tell. "Why don't you come home and we'll figure something out? I'm craving Chinese or sushi now that you said Asian. There's a strip mall a few miles below Frenchtown on the Jersey side that has a Chinese-Japanese buffet."

"That sounds great! A handsome date *and* sushi! What more could a girl ask for?"

"I could think of a few things," he said, raising one eyebrow slightly.

"Hey, you two! Do you not see me in the room?" Karen bellowed from the sink. Her smile was lifting her glasses off her nose. "I've got to get. Can you bring me home a quart of general kung pao chicken? I'm working late on a special project," she said, grabbing her purse as she flew out the door.

Tristan came up behind Lissa, who was gathering the dishes. He wrapped his arms around her and kissed her neck. "Thank you for breakfast."

"Can you be late for work?" she said, turning to face him with a large smile.

"I know it's a Saturday, but I have all of the crews showing up today. Everyone wants to finish up on time for the extra bonus. We're almost there." He bent down and kissed lips that still tasted of orange juice. "Ahhh, now that is delicious!"

She wrapped her arms around him tighter and kissed him deeply. "Yes, this is delicious."

She dressed for a day of dirty scrubbing, selecting two tee shirts, a hoodie, and jeans—the standard Melissa-wear. She went to the Glass Chopstick and jumped right in like she had been there many times before. Chef Jack was glad to see her. He had his fifteen-year-old son helping out.

"This is Art, my son. Art, this is Chef Mel."

"Hey, nice to meetcha. Cool name!"

"Thanks. No soccer today?" Mel said, noticing his tee shirt sporting a cartoon of a Pele kick.

"Hey, how did you know? We have a week off before playoffs. We're in first place in our division," he said with a proud grin on his face.

"Hey, you two, we've got a lot to get done!" yelled Chef Mark from across the kitchen and Frisbeed a piece of cardboard box toward them.

"Ok Dad!"

❖

Chapter Forty-One

Present Day

Lissa met Tristan at the house. They kissed, hugged, and caressed. They loved kissing each other. They wanted to make love, but they both knew they would be there all night and would never leave to have dinner, and Karen was expecting the chicken. When they got back, Tristan left the brown bag on the counter, complete with chopsticks, sauce, egg rolls, and tea. He grabbed Lissa by the hand and pulled her upstairs. As soon as he had her in his bedroom, he was hugging her and kissing her. Their lovemaking always took a long time because Tristan enjoyed touching every part of her; he was very much into foreplay. They had just reached an exciting climax together when they heard the front door open and the sound of Karen kicking her shoes off.

"Anyone home?" she called.

They joined her in the kitchen a few minutes later. Lissa warmed up the Chinese food for Karen while she went through the mail.

"So what are you two up to tonight?"

They both giggled and said, "Just dinner" and "Ya know, stuff."

"What should the three of us do tomorrow?" Lissa wondered. "We could finish cleaning the still and start pulling it out to polish it, or we could go shop a flea market in search of 1920 gun moll stuff."

"Sorry, I have church in the morning and I promised to take one of our senior ladies out to the diner for an early dinner. It's the highlight of her week. I'll be home later, though."

"Sorry, lass, I too have a job to finish up. You could come with me. I won't have all of the crews working. I'm just going to sweep up and spackle and cover nail holes in my woodwork."

"Well, I guess I'll go over to the Glass Chopstick and see if they could use me. If not, I'll come help you out. Is that okay, Trist?"

"Why, of course it is."

"I'll figure out what to put with chicken breast and make us a fine dinner."

❖

Chapter Forty-Two

Present Day

M el got to the Glass Chopstick by nine o'clock. Today they were to start unpacking dishes and stocking them for service. Everything had to be washed. Mel and Art decided to jump in to the project and let Mark straighten the walk-in to his liking. Art stuck his iPod into a speaker base and started cranking it up to the latest hip hop station.

"Is this music okay for you, Mel?"

"Oh yeah, sure; it's cool."

"Let's see your shirt today," Mel said.

He unzipped his hoodie all the way and displayed his shirt to her. It was a white tee shirt with a modern black pen-and-ink drawing of a soccer player.

"Hey, that's pretty neat-looking."

They got to work unloading cases of dishes, racking them and sending them through the dishwasher. The dry dishes were stacked upon a stainless steel table. They got a rhythm going and were almost done by noon.

They stopped for a cold drink and a slice of pizza that Mark had ordered. Lissa asked how school was going for Art. He said it was okay.

"Just okay? Are you in any special classes or programs? Are you a junior this year or next year?"

"I'm on the soccer team, and swimming starts soon. I like that. In English we just finished playing with oxymorons. Do you know what they are?"

"Whatcha call me? *Pretty ugly.*"

"No, ma'am, it's a *definite maybe,*" he laughed, showing pizza in his teeth.

"Oh, yeah, *exact estimate.*"

"I'll see you and raise it to *clearly misunderstood.*"

"Icy hot."

"Resident alien."

"You've been *found missing*!" she said, pointing at him.

"Umm, umm, *sanitary landfill,*" he mumbled.

"Butt head," she giggled, throwing the pizza crust away.

"That deserves a *silent scream.*"

"Well, we better get back to our *working vacation*!" she jumped off the stool and gave Art a high five.

"You're a pretty smart dog," she said, taking clean plates over to the gleaming stainless steel service line.

They got the glassware done, polishing it and putting it on trays. Bartenders were still putting away bottles and categorizing wines. They were able to get the flatware done and polished and put into containers for service. Even though she had done several hotel openings in the past, this was a good sample of what was expected of her in a few months. She might even ask Art to come over and help her, if his dad and soccer weren't keeping him busy.

That night she made mushroom-smothered chicken breast in a garlic wine sauce, and red pepper couscous on the side with fresh broccoli.

❖

Chapter Forty-Three

Sally, 1921

B y 1921, Sally had downsized the farm. She didn't want to work so hard. She was lonely. She put up grape jelly and a few bottles of wine for herself because Kings Road Winery wasn't buying grapes since the Eighteenth Amendment had gone into effect. It was the best way for her to use up the grape crop. She decided to socialize more and went to Sam asking for a job as a waitress. He was very patient with her in the beginning as she fumbled along, but she caught on quickly. She was now his head waitress. They got along great.

Jake pulled in as usual for his delivery of pork to Sam. He came in the back door, followed by a short stocky man who wore a big smile. Sally glanced quickly over at the two men and said hi. She was rushing some sweet tea to a table of four. When she was done taking their order, Sam introduced Jake's dad to her.

"Sally, this is Scott, Jake's dad. He brought him along to show him his route."

"Nice to meet you! Are you staying for lunch?" Sally said with a smile, putting a tray of pulled pork and cornbread platters together.

Scott looked up at her. He had the most amazing blue eyes that Sally had ever seen.

"Yes, I sure am hungry watching all of this delicious food go past. Jake, can we stay for a minute and catch a bite with this fine woman?"

"Why don't you eat, Pop, while I unload the meat? Order me something to go, and I'll eat on the run. You know what the wife is like if I don't get in at a decent time," Jake said as he headed to the door with Sam.

"Sally, I guess I'm yours," Scott said, gesturing with both arms stretched out.

"Let me show you where to park it, honey."

Scott ordered a chicken barbeque sandwich and told Sally to make up something that Jake would like. When he was finished eating, she put the check on the table and asked him how everything was.

He said, "It was the best sandwich and the best service that I've ever had." He smiled broadly at her, which raised his big cheeks up until his blue eyes squinted. He came up to the register with the change in the palm of his hand. Sally reached her hand out for the change. He put his hand out and glided his hand across hers so that she felt the curve of his hand. She felt a slight shudder deep inside from his touch.

"I know we just met, but if you're free some night, I would love to take you to a Valentino movie. Would you like that? Any movie. Whatever you like," he said, putting on his best boyish smile.

She hesitated at first. "Ahh, yes, I guess that would be nice. Saturday night would be fine. Let me get this order out to the table. Just a second." She ran into the kitchen thinking feverishly, Do I want to date? Is he really interested in me? She worried as she grabbed her order for another four-top. She glanced up and saw Jake and Sam coming through the back door.

She dropped the food off and came back to Scott, who was eyeing her as she worked. She had an urge to check her hair and make sure it was in place. Instead she put her hand up to her ample bosom and adjusted the collar of her dress. Why am I so nervous? she thought. "Okay, yes; do you want to pick me up?"

Should I have him for dinner? she deliberated. Oh, I can't do this.

Scott said, "We're going to your house next to pick up something," he said with a wink only seen by her. "So I'll know where you live. How's six o'clock sound to you? Is that too early?"

"As long as it is 6:00 p.m. and not a.m.," she said with a very toothy, cute smile. She passed him her phone number on a slip of paper.

The rest of the day, Sally hummed her favorite tune and giggled at jokes from the regulars. She was in such a good mood that one of the regulars pulled Sam over to tell him she might be on the sauce today. It wasn't usual for Sally to be as happy as a schoolgirl. She liked it. The day went by faster. Two days to go before she met Scott. She thought, Boy, he had nice eyes. And what a smile, she thought, with a large grin on her face.

❖

Chapter Forty-Four

1922

Dick Shutter was secretly watching the pork delivery. Everything seemed normal here. He had even watched them from his room when he had stayed there. Normal, but he knew something was up. It just wasn't right out in the open. It was just a feeling. He was hoping it wasn't the same wrong conclusion that he had when they had raided the Mauri farm. He thought that he had good evidence in the purchase trace out at the Mauri farm. He really wanted that to go down so his boss would stop yelling at him every week.

Sam was harder to do a grocery trace on, for he had no idea how much sugar and corn went into running his restaurant, so he wasn't sure how to track the ingredients. So if Sam was the major supplier, then he would have to follow everyone involved with him. Yesterday, he had followed the dairy guy for half a day with no leads. The day before that, it was the produce guy. He still had a chicken guy to follow tomorrow. After all, he was only one man. How hard did they expect him to work on just five-fifty a day?

He followed the Liberty Pork truck out of town, heading south to Lower Black Eddy. The road ran close to the river here, as the canals didn't start for a few more miles south. The canal was mainly used when the water and currents ran rough, or at long bends in the river. The truck made a right and then a left at the top of the hill. He tried not to follow so closely. He slowed his pace down a bit. It got rather hilly here, and he didn't want to lose them. He came over a small incline in the road just in time to catch the truck halfway down a dusty farm road. It doesn't look like a restaurant or a pig farm, he thought. I wonder what they are up to.

Dick drove straight ahead and pulled his car over behind a clump of trees. He got out and made his way through the brush to get a better look at what they were up to. A sense of hope coursed through his veins. It had started out being a sunny day, but it was now looking cloudy and getting grey, although it was only midday. The wind, he noticed, was starting to kick up also. He buttoned up his black wool jacket and thought that it was time to purchase a warmer black overcoat soon.

The Liberty Pork truck pulled up to the barn. A new man that he had never seen before got out and fumbled with a padlock and chain. Why would anyone lock a barn? he thought with a leering smile on his small round face. The wind took the door of the barn and for just a few seconds, he could see inside of it. It was dark in the interior, but he thought that he had noticed crates. He rubbed the palms of his small hands together with a "gotcha now" anticipation and also because the weather was changing quickly. The temperature had just dropped a few degrees. Then he wiped the corners of his lips.

I'll have to come back later tonight. This time I want to see for sure before I call Captain Jack down. "Yes!" he said aloud to the now-swaying brush.

❖

Chapter Forty-Five

1922

Scott was amazed at the volume of crates that his son and friends had accumulated. He was a little nervous for Jake. If his son ever got caught, he would be sentenced to a minimum of two years. But it was completely amazing to him that the operation was so well-controlled. Before this, he had only read about stuff in the paper. The *Philadelphia Bulletin* was constantly featuring stories about bootleggers. He didn't think the paper favored the law. They never took the side of the G-Men in their articles. One of their ace reporters had been arrested in a speakeasy raid one time. He had read about it, he remembered.

Scott opened the doors to the barn wide enough so that the truck could back in. This was pretty smart, he thought, so that anyone driving by couldn't see what they were doing. He was hoping that he would see Sally again. She had a nice property. It was a very clean and organized property—one that had been cared for over the years. Her barn was even clean and organized, with assorted tools nailed to the walls. Axes, wheat sickles, shovels, rakes—everything lined up by size and hung nicely.

Jake came around and opened the doors to the truck and started handing the empty crates to his dad. "Dad, I'm really glad to be hanging out with you," he said.

"Me too, son; I really liked Sally, also," he said with a big grin and started to sing, "She is one cat's meow."

"Yes, Dad, she is." Jake shook his head and rolled his eyes.

Then he told his dad to pick up the full crates.

Jake placed the full booze crates as far back in the truck as he could position them. The blocks of ice were slid in front of them. He put the full crates of pork that still had to be delivered to the door side. He also took a few of the empty crates, putting them behind the yet-to-be-delivered pork. If he were stopped, an immediate search of his truck would show nothing. It was the thought of getting caught with the booze that frightened him. His wife, although she enjoyed the extra money, would be furious and raise a ruckus with the police.

Scott helped his son. He was so proud of him for the work he was doing, legal or illegal. He was proud of his daughter-in-law and loved his grandchildren. He was most definitely happy to help his son out.

Scott had been a bricklayer most of his life. He felt like he had built most of the city. He had primarily lived and worked between downtown and the Walnut Hill section. He had seen many changes to the city in his fifty-two years. His body was tired now, and he was only working two or three days a week. His shoulders weren't what they used to be. His boss knew his knowledge of bricks and his speed at mudding up a wall. He had hired young laborers to help Scott out, and they did, but he was still very tired by the third day.

Presently, Scott noticed that the wind had picked up. The breeze blew in and slammed the barn door against the truck. It startled Jake for a minute. "Must be a storm coming in," he said.

"Yeah, look at how fast those clouds are moving in."

"Grab that last full case, and we'll get going to our last stop. Maybe we'll beat the storm into the city."

❖

Chapter Forty-Six

1922

Sally finally finished work at 4:30. The last table took forever to finish up, and then she had to clean up. She had filled her sauce jars and salt and peppers while she was waiting for them to vamoose. Her plan was to run over to Stella's Beauty Shop at the edge of town. She wanted the works from Stella. She never ever stopped in to see her and wasn't even sure of her hours. It was time to look more updated and pretty, she thought with a pursed lip. It had been so very, very long since anyone had noticed her—maybe not caring for herself was the reason why.

When she approached Stella's shop, which used to be a dentist's office back in the day, she got a little worried that it might be closed. There weren't any cars in the lot next to the house. She banged on the door, getting a little nervous. Nervous about going through with such a crazy idea and nervous that Stella couldn't take her.

Stella came to the door with a pink rubber curler in her hand. "Come on in, Sally. I'm in the middle of un-doing a perm for Mrs. Fritz, the librarian."

Sally thought, golly gees—even the widowed librarian tries to look pretty. She followed Stella into the back room.

"What can I do for you, Sally? Whatcha sellin'?" Stella said with a fag hanging off the side of her lip. Her hair was very dark, brownish black, slicked down with razor-cut bangs in a very hip Hollywood jazz bob. Red lipstick covered the edge of the paper on the homemade cigarette. How did she stay so thin, Sally wondered. She looks so good in her shift dress.

Sally was wondering if she should go so far with such a drastic modern look like Stella.

"I was just wondering if I could get a bob and a brunette rinse to cover my grey."

"I can do ya tomorrow. Can't do ya today. The mister is taking me to that new Scaramouch movie. I just love that actor Raymond or Rich, what's his name?"

"Yes, so do I," Wanda Fritz said, holding her hand out to retrieve yet another curler from Stella. She had a basket in her lap that she was placing them in. "His name is Ramón Navarro. A gorgeous species of male as I've ever seen! Almost as good-looking as Rudy Vallee. He played in *The Prisoner of Zenda*. Did you see it? What a great movie plot! He was one of the henchmen who gave the king a bottle of drugged wine. I mean Ramón, not Rudy. I read the book several times when I was younger.

"I read the book *Scaramouche*, also. What a story, I tell you—and then to have it made into a movie! *The Prisoner of Zenda*, I mean. Wow, I wish someone would ask *me* to go to see it. Well, maybe with this new perm. The mailman, Frank. You know Frank; he stops in the library every day and waits till I get to the counter to personally hand me the mail. I think he likes me, but he's afraid to ask me out. Sometimes I make him cookies. Maybe he's afraid that I might turn him down. I think he's just as cute as that Mexican actor Ramón Navarro. He's been turning up in a lot of movies lately. Don't you, I mean. . . . "

Before she caught her breath to continue, Sally spoke up fast. "How about tomorrow at 2:30? I gotta run and find a new dress. I don't want anything too exotic but something a little more updated."

"Sure, we'll see you then."

"Have you seen the new dresses at the Woolworth's, in New Hope? They had some with a sheer chiffon fabric over them. I just bought one in grey with wide pleats at the hem, low-cut in the front, so daring. I'm going to wear it tomorrow. I hope Frank sees it. I was just wondering if—"

Sally interrupted quickly before Wanda went into another breathless rant, "Why don't you ask Frank out? Forget the old rules. It's 1922, for God's sake. I have to run. Thanks, Stella. Good luck, Wanda!"

She got back into her Model-T and prayed that it would turn over right away. She wanted to get to New Hope to get one of those new-style dresses. She only owned black waitress dresses or cotton dresses.

She wanted to get back home before dark. It looked as if a storm was starting to brew. Brew, she thought. She could use a small nip of something. Her nerves were shot with all this fluff stuff.

It was almost eight o'clock when she pulled into her quiet, very dark farm. She really should leave a light on, but most of the time she was home by dark. She had spent all of yesterday's and that day's tips. She got a very nice dress with new lightweight sheer fabric over a rayon shift. She thought that it helped smooth her shapely figure a little. It was two shades of blue. No floral or prints for her.

Then she had to try on shoes and maybe a new triple-beaded necklace with blue tint. And then she found an adorable purse in the same shade. She even bought some new foundation, just to complete the package. It took her a while to decide if it was too much for an old farmer/waitress like her. She thought, Oh, what the hell, and then headed over to cosmetics. She figured it was about time to live it up. She didn't think that it would go very far. It was only a date to go to a movie, after all.

Next she stopped at the American Pacific grocery store at the edge of

New Hope. She bought a few items that she would never have bought for just herself. She went a little crazy, not knowing what Scott liked to eat, other than chicken barbeque. She almost couldn't wait until her new look was done. She didn't feel tired at all; a bit of adrenalin was coursing through her. She wanted to bake a cake as soon as she got home. Men always liked cake. She was also going to make a cheesy chicken casserole recipe that she had found on a saltine cracker box. Men loved cheese.

She took her hair out of the bun, and it flowed all the way past her bosom. Sally didn't pin it back, wanting to enjoy her last day with long hair. She baked and cleaned her house until well after ten. The drizzle had started at nine o'clock or so, and now it was a full hard rain. Her chocolate cake turned out beautifully. She made some boiled icing that came out perfect. Things were going well, and she didn't think she had been this happy in so many years, she couldn't remember. She was relentlessly humming to herself. She had even forgotten her nightly glass of wine.

It was almost eleven as she made her way up the dark stairs to her room. She didn't need a light. She had grown up in this house and knew every inch of it in the dark. As she felt for the round light switch on the wall of her bedroom, she noticed headlights turning into her driveway. The lights were quickly diminished. A streak of nature's bright lightning confirmed that an old Ford was coming up to her house. Her happy day was suddenly filled with terror. Was somebody coming to harm her? She wished Sam or Jake or Scott were there.

Gun, where is my gun? she thought, putting her hand up to her bosom and buttoning her top button with one hand. She looked out again and could catch the car down at the edge of the barn. She left the lights off in the house. She went over to her dresser, and under some very old corsets she found her little .45 caliber gun. She used to keep it in the barn for dying animals and prey animals, but now they were all gone.

Sally felt a chill run through her. She pulled on one of Stan's old raincoats and his galoshes and held the gun firmly in front of her. She was walking quietly and bravely for a woman alone. She came around the side of the barn. She inched along quietly. Someone was opening the door of the barn, and she heard the chain drop.

Her heart was beating twice its normal speed now. Who could be in there? She knew everyone in town and had never had anything stolen from her. It must be a revenuer. Maybe it was that little bug man, she thought. As she came around the corner, thunder clapped loudly and the wind blew the barn door open wide. It banged loudly against the side. Lightning followed just as she came through the door, entering the barn.

❖

Chapter Forty-Seven

1922

He was a little nervous about doing this. He had never broken into anyone's place before. It was dark out and raining like crazy. I'll probably see a mouse or a rat and scream, he thought. He hated little scurry things. He should have just packed up and moved back home like he had been thinking all week. I'm not going anywhere up here, he thought, and I'm not going anywhere down home. He was so tired of the bullies from high school that still came into the store, taunting him. That was why he had left and why he hesitated to go back.

If only they could see him now. He was going to be the big man at the office, judging by the number of crates around him. He used a match and was hoping for a streak of lightning so he could find a crowbar to pry the wooden lid off the box. He certainly wasn't prepared for this job—no flashlight, no tools, and no raincoat. Where was his head? He was just lucky that the lock had popped so easily, like it wasn't closed tightly.

The lightning flashed and he saw a huge man coming at him with long grey hair streaked against his face by the rain. He was holding a gun with both hands.

Sally said hoarsely, "Who are you and what are you doing on my property? I called the sheriff and he's on his way."

Dick screamed, a high-pitch, startled scream. He stood up as straight as he could, to appear taller. He didn't even have a gun on him. "Treasury Agent Shutter here, G-Man. Please put the gun down. You are under arrest for the violation of the Volstead Act of 1919 and the Eighteenth Amendment." Why did I say that? he wondered. Like anyone really cared at this point.

"Oh, really, you little bug. You've annoyed me for the last time. Those boxes are empty, so I guess you are mistaken," Sally said and pulled the trigger. Thunder struck again at the same moment. She pulled the trigger again. Nothing happened. "Damn it," she yelled.

Dick thought, Oh my God! I am being shot at by a woman—or is it a man? Did they miss?

Soon to follow the thunder was a huge bolt of lightning. Sally glanced at the wall of tools in that instant of light. She quickly dropped the gun that she had forgotten to put bullets in. She reached out for the wheat sickle.

Dick was about twenty yards away from her. He wasn't shot yet, and he didn't want to get hurt. He hated pain. He just wanted to get out of the barn and go back to being a clerk. This job certainly didn't pay enough to warrant his life. He started inching toward the crazy person with the witch-like hair. She turned to get something, and he started to make a dash for it. He wanted to get as far away as he could. The heck, by golly, with being a G-Man; he wasn't cut out for it.

Within seconds, she had the sickle in her hand. It was resting on two cut nails. She lifted the sickle, which came down quickly into her hands. The shape and curve was designed for fast, even swinging. She heard something move behind her. She turned quickly, the sickle lower now. She came around and sliced the forehead of the little man. He was bleeding and screaming. Should she help him, or should she tell him to run? The crates were empty anyway, she knew. She hadn't done anything wrong to Congressman Volstead.

"You better run fast and get out of my barn and get off my property!" she screamed in the loudest voice she had used since Stan had been alive.

Dick Shutter beat feet.

She held the wheat sickle firmly. I could have killed the man, she thought. I've done it before. She suddenly felt better, empowered almost. The reality of what she had just done hadn't sunk in yet. She would be in big trouble. She had lied about calling the sheriff just to sound important and not alone. She had just wounded a government officer. She could be sent up the river for a lot more time than if she sold a bottle. Suddenly, she had the urge to go to the bathroom. Hearing a low moan, it took a minute to realize it was coming from her. She noticed that she was still holding the sickle and slowly rested it against some crates as if it were suddenly heavy and then took a deep breath.

Sally felt around in the pocket of the raincoat and found a little pint bottle that Stan had hid along with a hanky. Sally popped off the cork and took a big swig of the warm, harsh whiskey. She took the hanky, wiped her sickle off till it looked brand-new, and hung it back on the cut nails.

She took a look around in the almost pitch-black barn. Her eyes had adjusted well to the dark. She went over to a crate and slid the top off. Just as she thought, they were empty. She felt around the floor of the barn for the useless gun. I'll put it back under the corsets and put the bullets in it for next time, she thought.

❖

Chapter Forty-Eight

1922

D ick heard screaming but didn't know where the scream was coming from. It was him. He ran to his car and started the engine. Thank God it started! His screaming turned to a whimper and then a whine from the pain. Blood was everywhere. He wasn't sure if he had wet himself. Will my brains fall out? he thought. Where is the closest hospital? North or south? He wasn't sure. Was he in shock? He didn't know. Where did his glasses get to? Adrenalin was keeping him going. The gash was across the right side of his forehead. He thought he was going to die. It felt huge. She tried to kill me! She tried to kill me! She tried to kill me!

He quickly drove out of her driveway. The rain had Dick pretty soaked, making even more of a bloody mess. He was driving pretty fast, trying to remember which way to turn to get to the main road.

Finally he made it. He made a right towards Philadelphia, towards civilization, and towards Captain Jack. He wasn't seeing well without his glasses and with the rain coming down so heavily on the windshield. The wipers weren't moving the rain off fast enough. One speed was all his entire car offered. He was speeding and driving with one eye.

He needed a hospital. He needed to cover his wound. With what? he thought. He started to take off his overcoat. The road turned, and he swayed into the other lane. He managed to get off his overcoat and attempted taking off his jacket. He figured he could put the jacket around his head. The blood gushed more every time he moved his hand off the wound. Maybe he should just keep holding it. He swerved again and straightened out.

He was coming into a section of road that ran right along the river. Lightning shot through the sky, illuminating the racing current. He glanced at it quickly, only seeing a muddy blur without his glasses. He let go of his forehead again and pulled another sleeve of his jacket off. There was blood all over the steering wheel. The old wooden wheel was slippery. He was now sitting on both jackets, even though they were released from his arms.

Around the next bend in the road, he passed a slow-moving vehicle going the opposite direction. He noticed that his eyes were getting even blurrier. His vision was closing in on him. The other vehicle passed him, and he veered into their lane, missing them by what seemed like inches. He pressed on the brakes, trying like hell to focus on what was in front of him. It was a big wide muddy field. No! he thought just as his car plunged into the rushing Delaware River.

He was immediately jolted into this new sensation. He needed to get out of his car quickly. He lifted the door lever up and pushed; he pushed again, and again. Water was everywhere and rising fast. His car was moving quite quickly with the strong current. He pushed again and the door budged open. Now what to do? He held onto the door. The car wasn't sinking just yet. If he let go, he might be taken under with the strong current.

Chapter Forty-Nine

1922

A car stopped by the side of the road. Frank, the driver, jumped out and ran to the edge. A streak of lightning confirmed that a car had been taken by the current.

"Did you see that, Mabel?" he said to his wife, who had just joined him at the edge.

"I think that car went right into the river!" she said, pulling the collar up on her overcoat.

"What should we do?" Frank said, rubbing his damp hair with his fingertips.

"Well, Pa it's almost midnight. Kinda late. How 'bout we drive up till we see a house with lights on?"

"I think I seen one back a bit, Ma," he said, putting the car in gear. He wiped his forehead as raindrops started falling from his hair. "I shoulda put my hat on. Let's go back."

Mr. and Mrs. Frank Parks sat for an hour in a farmhouse about four-tenths of a mile south of where they had witnessed the car plunge in. The old farmer was patient—said he wasn't much of an early bird anyway. A sheriff and an officer from the local town showed up minutes behind each other. They left a report of all that had happened, which wasn't much. They left their telephone number and went on their way.

The officers gathered outside the old man's home and suggested driving up and down the river a few miles with the spotlight just in case they might see anyone still alive. All they found were the tire tracks leading into the river.

The storm was starting to subside. They had no luck finding the car, and no bodies were recovered. They figured they'd have an easier search in the daylight, provided that the flooding didn't get too bad as the day progressed.

❖

Chapter Fifty

1922

Sally went in to work like she did any other day. Today was a very different day, though. Sally wore a smile on her face. She didn't let anyone know why she was so happy or how excited she was about her new date, new hair, new dress, new shoes, and so on. She kept thinking of all of the possibilities.

But she did have an occasional fleeting moment when she wondered what happened to the bug man that she had squashed the previous night.

She ran from work that afternoon as soon as the lunch rush was over, forgetting to fill the salt and peppers and to check the sauces. Ahh, let the young people do it for a change, she reflected. She was at Stella's shop twenty minutes before the appointment with great excitement in her heart. Sally sat for a few minutes looking at Hollywood magazines and hairstyle sketch books. She found a few sketches and showed them to Stella.

"Let's get you fixed up, girl. I want to create something with layers to bring out those natural curls. It'll be easy for you to manage," she said while un-pinning Sally's bun. "We'll also magically give you back your natural hair color. Are you ready?"

"You bet I am! I want to be the cat's meow," she purred in her best kitty voice, wearing a big smile. This was fun! This was living!

It only took an hour and twenty minutes. The cost was thirty-five cents for the bob and seventy-five cents for the hair color. She couldn't believe how pretty she looked. Stella even put makeup on her cheeks and lips that brought out her eyes. She also pulled and trimmed Sally's eyebrows and then penciled them in to define them more.

She headed home, sitting up straight and proud. She started singing on the way back to the farm. This was something she never did. She had no plans tonight. She pulled into her yard and found a truck sitting by the barn.

"Oh, crap!" she said aloud. She jumped out of her car, approaching the barn with a good pace.

"Sally, is that you? Holy macaroni! If it wasn't for the uniform, I wouldn't have recognized you. You look great! What did you do to yourself in such a short time? You really look great. I don't ever remember you looking so great. I mean, did you have something that you forgot to tell me today? I found a pair of bloody glasses that look like they used to belong to the revenuer." Sam was never one to mince words and usually got right to the point. He cocked his head to one side, expecting an explanation from her.

"I didn't kill him, Sam; I didn't kill him. I should have, but I didn't. I don't know what happened to him, either. I've been so busy today that I kinda forgot about him." She cocked her head and smiled puckishly. "I don't think you should leave any booze here for the time being until we hear what happened to him."

"Start from the beginning, Sally. What exactly happened?" Sally and Sam took a seat on the wooden crates, and she explained the events that led up to the bloody dismissal. A few times she used her hands to demonstrate, especially when it came time for the sickle part of the story.

"Are you all right, Sally? You are the bravest person I know. About what time did this happen?" Sam said, patting her on the back.

Sally told him.

"Then our troubles might be over. They found a car washed up on the Jersey side of the Scudder Falls sand bar near Wilburtha. You know, right under the Scudder Falls Bridge. It was covered over by water last night, but today a car that sounded like Dick Shutter's was found sitting on the middle of the sand. Old Mr. and Mrs. Parks saw it go in. They were on their way home from her mother's house. She's been awfully ill lately. Mabel doesn't think her mother will make it through the winter."

Sally had her hand on her ample chest again while she listened to Sam's story.

"I'll call Bill up at the Village Tavern and see if he has seen him around today."

"So they haven't found his body, Sam?"

"I don't know yet, Sally. I guess you're right about me not keeping the booze here for a while. I can keep it piling up in my secret basement. When we find out if this guy is dead or alive; then we'll know which way to go with the hooch. How big was that gash?"

"He'll probably be pretty mad at me. I put at least a two-inch gash in his forehead. He acted like his brains were falling out," she said, stroking her neck with her hand and wishing for a cigarette.

"I'm sure there will be an investigation and a few people asking around if he is found dead. Just play it like you don't know anything," Sam said.

"Okay, Sam; sorry for the trouble."

"Are you kidding? Thank you for being so brave and standing up to the bug."

"Do you want to come in for a sip of wine?"

"No, thanks; Abbey will be waiting on me. It'll be dark soon, plus I have to unload this hooch back into the cellar tonight. I hope we hear something by Wednesday on this. We have another delivery scheduled to go out."

"Okay. See ya for lunch in the morning. Remember I get off right after rush. I have a date with Scott."

"Scott?" Sam said with a scratch to the top of his temple, not recalling the name in town.

"Jake's dad, Scott. He was here the other day."

"Oh, yeah! Now I remember. Yes, he is a nice guy. You deserve a nice guy in your life, Sally."

"Thanks, Sam. See you tomorrow."

❖

Chapter Fifty-One

Present Day

Monday morning turned out to be a dreary, rainy day. Karen checked the Internet that morning and said that a slow-moving green blob would hover over the area all day, the worst part hitting after ten. Funny, Melissa thought, how weather is decided by the color. Better than an orange stormy day or a pink snowy day, she thought. Thinking of color, she contemplated about her restaurant and decided to run all colors of sugar in reproduction pressed-glass sugar jars. She should have pink, green, yellow, and blue artificial sugar and natural brown and white sugar packets of real sugar. How nice that would be.

The sugar inspiration led her into the basement with a large cup of coffee in hand. Karen and Tristan were already out the door. She did want to go over to help the boys at the Glass Chopstick, but something was telling her to stay home and take care of stuff for herself. The new help was supposed to start, and she felt it better to stay out of the way. Most of the dirty work was done. The new staff just had to start making it happen. Food would start getting delivered this week, and they should be open by next Monday. Waiters had to set up the coffee stations; fill ketchup bottles, creamers, salts, peppers; fold linen; and prep the dining area. She would go back at night near the grand opening and help with prep and menu layout. There were always last-minute menu issues. She was good at the details like that.

In the basement, she stared at the still. She decided that it was a perfect day for a big project. She took one more sip of coffee, rubbed the palms of her hands on her jeans, and started figuring out where to start in the dismantling of the still. She took another sip of coffee and ran upstairs to find a flat screwdriver in the kitchen drawer.

It was approaching one o'clock when Lissa realized that she hadn't had breakfast and the coffee was gone. She washed her hands, and a few minutes later, she was enjoying microwaved couscous and broccoli. She looked around the kitchen. It was covered with rags, towels, and pieces of brass and steel. She remembered the battle of taking one large piece up to the hallway tub to clean it. As she was scooping up the last of the couscous into her fork, she suddenly had a shuddering thought. Suppose I can't get it all back together?

She pulled some pork chops out of the freezer for dinner and started polishing the brass. It gleamed with imperial age. While she was cleaning, she came across a brass plaque. She had to scrub it before she could polish it. Some parts were easy to clean, and some parts were just disgusting, and all of them were smelly. Eventually, she could read the plaque. "For my beloved Abbey." It was Abbey's still, she thought. How beautiful it was that he had made the still for her! The most any guy had ever done for her was to copy his recipes for her, which was pretty nice, but later he had wanted her collection, too.

When Karen got home before Tristan, she almost dropped the mail. "What is this?"

"It's Abbey's still. Look," Lissa said, displaying the part with the inscription on it with her blackened fingertips.

"That's beautiful. The whole thing is beautiful. Where are we going to keep it? It looks so big all over the kitchen table."

"Gee, I don't know, but I was thinking that I could whip up some Cajun pork chops with bits of apples, some fresh veggies, and brown rice," Lissa said, knowing that the change in subject would help her from getting into more trouble.

"I guess you can put it back together in the parlor; that way if you need to move it, you can just go out the front vestibule doors. They're wide enough. We hardly ever go in the parlor."

Lissa ran over to her friend and gave her a big hug. They were both ample, and it often made for awkward hugs. "I love you, Karen, and thanks!"

"You better get cooking; I'm starved and I'm glad you are here, my ol' sock," she said, adjusting her glasses and picking up the pile of mail. "I need to check my email and pay some bills. I'll see you in a few minutes to help."

❖

Chapter Fifty-Two

Present Day

T he day was still sporting light patches of showers; the Internet showed light green dots across most of eastern Pennsylvania. It was a storm that came across from the west and was running out of steam. Lissa was still assembling the still in the parlor when the phone rang.

"Hello?"

"Hi, this is Anne Green, from Bucks County National. Is Melissa Star there?"

"Hi, Ms. Green. This is Lissa. What's up? Did you need more information from me?"

"Oh no, I think they had enough information. Congratulations, they approved your loan. Apparently one of the district officers caught a taste of your luncheon last week while he was in town picking up documents. You made quite an impression on the right guy. Plus Jim Burke gave an outstanding recommendation for you.

"We do have one problem, and frankly I have never seen this happen in the decade that I have worked in this department."

"Oh, no, what is it?" Melissa held her breath.

"Ms. Star, they feel you need more money than you had projected for the opening of your restaurant. I tell you, Ms. Star, I have never seen this done before. Actually, quite often they offer less money than asked."

"Wow." Melissa was now pushing her hair back with her hand and staring at a picture on the wall but not seeing it.

"The demographics for the area, the housing development projects that our bank is funding in your area, the taste of the food, the gimmick or idea for the establishment, and the respect of Jim Burke all were positive factors in the loan."

"Wow, this is wonderful!"

"So when can you come in and sign the papers? How about noon or one o'clock today?"

"Yes, oh yes; I'll be there at one o'clock. Do I need to bring anything?"

"Yes, bring your checkbook, and we will make a deposit for you."

She hung up the phone. She was so elated! She called the realtor next to get an update. The agent said that the owner had accepted her offer. He was just glad that he wouldn't have to watch the building stand idle. Mel said that she would be interested in a quick settlement. She asked if the closing could be put in order within a week.

Things are moving along yippee skippee, she thought. Then she got a little scared. She shook it off by telling herself that she had done this kind of work for so many years for other people and that she was more than ready to do it for herself with the help of her best friends.

❖

Chapter Fifty-Three

Present Day

The weeks seemed to go by so quickly for Melissa. She worked day and night in her building. She gutted walls, stripped old floor tiles, planned the kitchen layout, and reconfigured the bathroom to meet handicap codes. The plumbing alone would already be over the estimate, so she did as much of the dirty work as possible to keep the cost down. Tristan and Karen were there, and her brothers often helped her out on weekends.

By mid-November, she was starting to receive the major kitchen equipment, mostly pre-owned from the used restaurant supply house on Second Street in Philly. New reproduction glassware and dishes had started showing up. The dining room flooring was done. The still took up the center of the dining room. Soon the chairs would be in. They were also used and had to be painted. The tables were aged oak. She had found a supplier of used oak tables from farmhouses and schools. She was so happy with her find. She was also happy to be able to keep costs within budget—except for the plumber.

Mark and Art came by a few days to help out. Melissa couldn't believe it when she saw them. She said hi to Mark and said, "What do ya think, Art…pretty ugly?"

Mark's head moved slightly as if it was something he hadn't heard. Art said, "Definite maybe!" He high-fived Lissa, and then they did a street handshake which involved several different hand movements. Mark just watched the forward communication that Lissa was making with his son.

Jim Burke and his wife stopped in right before the grand opening. Lissa was hanging pictures that Karen had framed of Abbey and the family.

"You've done a spectacular job here, Melissa."

"It's so great to see you two," she addressed both Jim and Christy. "Thank you for coming! I'm so glad you stopped by. I've been meaning to thank you for the good word you put in for me at the bank."

"That was nothing," he said, reaching out to shake Lissa's hand. Christy was wearing a black and white sweater set with a rough pearl and crystal necklace. Melissa wore a paint-stained tee shirt and dirty jeans with a hole in the knee—but none of that mattered.

"It really looks great. I love your ideas for the theme, the name of the place. It really has been a buzz all around town."

"Thank you," Lissa beamed. "Wait until you see the uniforms that we've gotten. It was a little expensive, but I think it was needed to bring the place together. I even had to build a small locker room in the basement for the employees. Well, don't let me bore you."

"Oh, no, not at all. This is all very exciting!" Christy said. Jim was smiling and looking over at her. She was such a pretty woman.

"When is the grand opening?" Jim asked.

"I'm hoping that this Monday we can have a trial dinner, and I've advertised Tuesday as the grand opening. I would love it if you could make it. I also asked Chef Jake, Art, Chef Mark, a few people from the bank, and a few friends."

"We would love to come!" Christy and Jim both said.

Lissa had also invited some of Tristan's crew who had helped out with the construction, and the plumber. One VIP in attendance would be José, and she looked forward to meeting his wife.

Her chef was set to go, well-trained, and had worked in several types of kitchens, including a barbeque kitchen on the waterfront in South Philly. The waitresses would be in tomorrow to start training. They would be the first to try the menu so that Chef Kevin could practice. She wanted him to be on his own as much as possible, but she would and could jump behind the line at a moment's notice.

Life was good. She was exhausted at night, but it felt good. Lissa spent only a few sleeping hours at home. Tristan seemed to understand and really must have loved her a lot, because he was being very patient with her. He felt a small bite of being second in her life, but he thought about his work and how certain jobs consumed him. She had just fallen in love with her restaurant and was already finding it hard to love Tristan back. For now, they had no plans for love or the future.

The practice dinner was a great time for the staff and for Melissa's guests. There were a few glitches, but all were small and insignificant. Melissa had forgotten to plan for small children—milk, Hershey's syrup, and crayons. She did have a menu in place for them. They had also forgotten lemons on the smoked salmon salad. The chef performed to her expectations, and she wasn't required in the kitchen, which made for a delightful evening for her.

The next day, a tall plant arrived from Jim and Christy Burke for the grand opening. She also received a small bouquet of fresh flowers from her best friends on Rhoades Road. She also received a card from José and Ann Green.

Karen arrived right before the opening with a bow around the oak deacon's bench that she had purchased months ago. "I thought you needed something in the vestibule area in case you have a line of people or people waiting for take-out, ol' sock, ol' kid," Karen said, putting the bench down where it fit perfectly.

"Thank you, ol' pal—for the flowers, for your support, and for helping me with this crazy idea. Oh, and thank you for introducing me to Tristan," she said, putting her arms around Karen and giving her a big hug. "Now I need you to get the girls together for a brief meeting about specials. You're still going to hostess for me tonight, aren't you?"

"Of course! We've come a long way since Monongahela Junior High and Mr. Pallie's classes, haven't we?" They high-fived each other, touched knuckled fists, and finally did the pinky finger wrap; it was their secret handshake from long ago.

Karen headed into the kitchen to round up the wait staff.

Tristan came in a few minutes later and said, "If you have just a few minutes, I need to see you out front."

"Just a few minutes, Trist. I have to go over the dinner specials with the chef and staff and give them a big boost."

He took her by the hand and pulled her out the front door. "I just wanted to give you a big kiss and tell you how much I love you. I'm so proud of you, and you did this in such a short amount of time." He hugged and kissed her, and she returned the passion.

All was good at Still Smokin'.

❖

Chapter Fifty-Four

1922

S ally had a great day on Saturday. She noticed that her tips were higher than normal. Could it be from the smile, or the haircut and dye job? It didn't really matter; she was happy and couldn't wait until later that day. It was a pretty exciting week for her, and she noticed her clothes fitting a little more loosely. She had lost six pounds since Scott asked her out!

Scott called the restaurant at one o'clock. He said that he would be there at six o'clock, if it was okay. Sally said that if he could come at five o'clock, she would throw something together for them to eat before the movie. Little did he know the planning that she had put into the meal!

Sally greeted Scott promptly at five o'clock. "Come in! I'll show you around, and then we can eat," she said, trying not to be nervous. She did notice his right foot moving in a circle motion and guessed that he was nervous, too. He was holding his fedora very tightly.

She said, "Forgive me. Let me take your hat and coat." She offered a huge smile to reassure him. "Would you like a glass of wine? I made it myself."

"Absolutely. I mean, yes, I would love to have a bottle . . . I mean glass.

I can't believe how beautiful you look, Sally. You changed your hairstyle. I really like it. You also have a beautiful home. Show me around?"

The rest of the evening was full of compliments. He loved the cheesy chicken and cracker casserole. He loved the chocolate cake. It turned out to be his favorite, and he asked for a second slice, if she had more of that delicious coffee. She couldn't be more thrilled with him.

The movie that was planned never did materialize. When dinner was finished, they retired to the front parlor where he built a small fire in the river stone fireplace. They opened a second bottle of wine. The two sat and talked for hours until it was time to leave.

Sally was worried about the late hour, but Scott said that he had taken a room with Sam for the night. He would be okay. He also asked for a kiss good night. Daring as it seemed to Sally, she kissed him back several times, moving her hand to his waist.

He asked if he could see her in the morning. She said that would be fine. They could take a hike at Ringing Rocks Park. She hadn't been there in years. He said he had heard of it, but had never been there. Sally was thinking of packing a lunch.

❖

Chapter Fifty-Five

1922

The day was perfect, sunny with just a slight fall chill in the air. It was actually warm for that time of year. They walked and talked about their spouses, his kids, and the fact that she had never had any. They discussed career paths. He told her he never wanted to be a bricklayer, but it was something his father and uncle had taught him. It was expected of him to follow in this highly sought-after trade. He said that he would never force it upon his son. He said he was proud of his son. He was proud of his family and loved all of them. He especially loved his grandchildren, who called him G-Pa. Wasn't that cute?

They stopped a few times along the path and stared into each other's eyes. Sally really liked this man with his rough appearance and the strong arms. He was so sensitive. She didn't know men could be so sensitive. They found a nice rock formation and decided to put a blanket down and have their picnic lunch. He asked if she wanted to take in a movie again, and she giggled. She couldn't believe she had actually giggled. A movie would be nice. She didn't ask, but figured he would be staying another night above the restaurant.

He asked to see her the following weekend, if that was okay. She said that would be fine. He couldn't wait to see her again.

❖

Chapter Fifty-Six

1922

O n Tuesday morning, right before lunch, a sheriff and the local sheriff, Don Smith, stopped in to see Sam. "Hi Sam, this is Sheriff John Freemon out of the Bucks County office."

"Nice to meet you," Sam said, putting his hand out. "How you doing, Don? Your wife has been in a few times. She's doing great next door in Abbey's place."

"It's about a federal agent named Richard Shutter," Don said. "He often introduced himself by the name Dick Shutter."

"Oh yeah, he went missing about five days ago. Rumor has it that his car was found by Scudder Falls. Small-town news travels fast."

"Yeah, with Lucy the operator working, nothing stays quiet long," Don said with a slight smirk.

"When was the last time you saw him, Sam?"

"Last week or so, he was hanging around out back watching my delivery trucks for some strange reason. Dick thought I hadn't noticed him, but I know everything that goes on around my restaurant."

"How about Sally and the rest of your employees?" said Sheriff Freemon.

"You can ask them yourself. Rosie and Samantha are off today. I'll get Sally."

They asked Sally if she had seen him, and she answered just the same way that Sam had, that it had been about a week ago that he was hanging around in the alley. She had seen him watching the deliveries when she went out to light up a fag.

"Did you find him?" Sally asked.

"No, we think the current might have taken his body further south. Nothing has turned up yet. We found a lot of blood in the interior of the car, like he had hit his head. He also had a chunk of deer fur in his headlight, so we think he might have hit a frightened deer and run into the river."

"Poor little man, poor little man," Sally cooed, rubbing her hands on her upper arms and shaking her head. She went back to resetting tables.

❖

Chapter Fifty-Seven

1923

T he winter of 1923 turned out to be a mild one for the area. It sometimes happened when the fall brought many Nor'easters up the coastline. Sam's restaurant did well all winter. Christmas was spent with Sally; Sam; Abbey; Victor; Shirley; Auntie Adele; Jake, his wife Maxine, and his two kids, Margaret and John; and G-pa Scott. A great time was had by all. That New Year's Eve was celebrated at Sam and Abbey's with Adele and her new boyfriend, Scott and Sally, Jake and Maxine. They rang in the New Year hoping for one as good as 1923 had been. Sally brought bottles of wine, and Sam brought his Philadelphia bourbon.

In the spring, Sally was still seeing Scott. She had lost twenty pounds and had never been happier. They spent Sundays in Philadelphia with Jake's family, traveling back after an early Sunday dinner. She loved his grandchildren and the whole family experience. Scott and his family were becoming more like her family, like Sam and Abbey were.

Abbey purchased a small state-of-the-art Brownie camera. It was the first one she had ever bought herself. She said that she wanted more pictures of the kids, as they were growing so fast. One day she had it down at the restaurant taking shots of Sam working. Scott had stopped in and said, "Let me get a picture of the three of you out back."

Once outside, he said, "Here, stand by the window. Now everyone hold each other and smile." He cranked the little lever to wind the film in place and, holding it chest level, he said, "Okay, ready!"

Epilogue

In the summer of 1924, the Lanzetti brothers' gang was finally raided at a warehouse on Front Street, in Philadelphia. Captain Jack Blanchard led the band of G-Men into the raid, rushing the building from all entrances. The four Lanzetti brothers were starting to think that they were above the law. The police took them by surprise with minimum shooting and injury.

They were pouring gallons of booze down a drain when the press arrived. Pictures of Captain Jack axing cases of booze made the front page of the *Bulletin* and *Philadelphia Daily News*. Captain Jack wanted to make sure it made the news. He stayed in Philadelphia and continued his work.

As a result of the Lanzetti brothers raid, Sam and Jake lost their buyer. They decided that after three years of making illegal liquor, it was time to quit. Jake helped to make one final batch of hooch that summer. This was strictly for personal consumption.

Afterwards, they secured the room and screwed the bookcase to the stone wall with large brackets that Scott had picked up. They felt they had been pretty lucky. Jake and Sam both had enough college money put away for the kids. Sam had moved his money to a safe deposit box at the bank instead of under the front porch. They were also very fortunate to have such a close friendship.

A letter surfaced from Dick Shutter. He wrote to Captain Jack about how he was almost killed by a big crazy man-woman with long witch-like hair. She had yielded a huge ax at him and then sent him down the river. He had hung on to his car until the early light, when he was able to walk through waist-deep water over to the New Jersey shoreline. He made his way back to West Virginia and was requesting any severance pay if he could get it. Captain Jack had just laughed at the letter but was glad the little man was still alive and back in his home town. Jack decided to get his last paycheck and an extra one for his troubles, poor little guy.

Scott and Sally moved in together. They loved each other, but couldn't make the commitment to be married yet. They knew it was a scandalous thing to do, but it was happening in Hollywood all the time. They didn't care; they were happy.

Lissa moved in over her very successful restaurant in the spring. She spent every extra dime reinvesting in the business. She was able to write out weekly checks to repay all those who had helped her. Eventually, Tristan moved in with her. It was hard for him to leave Karen, but he needed to be with Lissa as much as her schedule would allow.

Karen started slowly seeing a widower from her church. They often met at Still Smokin' for a bite to eat after choir practice. He had two daughters and shared many interests with Karen. One of her daughters and granddaughter moved back in with her after her daughter's marriage had gone bad. Karen was very happy. She had the secret basement walls patched and sheet-rocked with the extra restaurant income. She turned the room into a cheery, spider free, playroom for her grandchildren.

It is not a card holiday; there are no costumes to buy, no decorations to be hung. People do not dye rivers green in celebration. It's a holiday that ended thirteen years of public disregard for a law. It's known as

Repeal Day because the Twenty-first Amendment repealed the Eighteenth Amendment on December 5, 1933. It was a long time ago, but a notable time in United States history, and is still celebrated at a few establishments. We take for granted the freedom to cook with wine or have a beer at a football game.

"The Freedom to Celebrate/Celebrate the Freedom."

–Unknown Author

CPSIA information can be obtained at www.ICGtesting.com
Printed in the USA
BVOW08s1601181113

336574BV00001B/2/P